NO BARRIERS

Erik Weihenmayer and Buddy Levy

NO BARRIERS

A Blind Man's Journey to Kayak the Grand Canyon

St. Martin's Griffin
New York

First published in the United States by St. Martin's Griffin,
an imprint of St. Martin's Publishing Group.

NO BARRIERS. Copyright © 2019 by Erik Weihenmayer and Buddy Levy. All rights
reserved. Printed in the United States of America. For information, address
St. Martin's Publishing Group, 120 Broadway, New York, NY 10271.

Foreword copyright © 2017 by Bob Woodruff.

www.stmartins.com

The Library of Congress Cataloging-in-Publication Data is available upon request.

ISBN 978-1-250-20677-0 (trade paperback)
ISBN 978-1-250-24772-8 (ebook)

Our books may be purchased in bulk for promotional, educational, or business use.
Please contact your local bookseller or the Macmillan Corporate and Premium Sales
Department at 1-800-221-7945, extension 5442, or by email at
MacmillanSpecialMarkets@macmillan.com.

First Edition: August 2019

10 9 8 7 6 5 4 3 2

To my father, Ed, who embodied No Barriers
before it had a name

—Erik

This is a true story,
though some names have been changed.

FOREWORD

By Bob Woodruff, ABC News

Chances are that at some point in our lives, we will all be tested. The possibilities are endless, and they read like a long list of what-ifs. Which is why the interesting part of any story is not necessarily the exact nature of the obstacles we meet, but in how we choose to respond.

It was an honor to be asked to write the foreword for *No Barriers: A Blind Man's Journey to Kayak the Grand Canyon* because this story and its author embody what it means to meet adversity and not let "the bad thing" define us. In short, to quote my wife, you make a choice to get "bitter or better."

My own challenging moment came in January 29, 2006, when I was covering the Iraq war outside of Baghdad for ABC News. While standing halfway out of a tank with my cameraman, a 125-mm roadside bomb exploded, leaving me with a traumatic brain injury (TBI) and vastly changing the direction of my life.

. . .

The blast shattered my skull, embedding rocks and other debris in my body and shattering my shoulder bone. But none of the other injuries mattered. They would heal. It was the TBI, the signature wound of these wars, that would prove to be my greatest obstacle. I would spend the next few years struggling to put my cognitive abilities back together, returning to my job as a journalist, and working harder than I ever had in my life.

Immediately following the blast, my cameraman, Doug Vogt, and I were flown from Iraq to Germany, then on to National Naval Medical Center in Bethesda where I spent thirty-six days in a coma. When I finally woke up and began to understand the enormity of what I had lost, it was my family and friends who surrounded me, along with the other military families, all on the same journey, experiencing firsthand the devastation and legacy of war up close and at home.

I am a journalist, and although I had understood the probability that I could be killed, I had spent very little time thinking about severe injury. My injury catapulted me into a world I had never seriously considered or contemplated. And from that tragedy, many positive things have resulted. I have been proud to use my story to help others traveling along the same road.

There is nothing courageous about my story. Hundreds of thousands of our troops who have volunteered to go to Iraq and Afghanistan when their country asked have returned home with both physical and invisible injuries. Unlike me, working for a news organization that cared for me and my family with unlimited rehabilitation and resources, many of our military families may not have access to the same level of resources all the way through. Not all of them have friends and family at home like I did to root for me and pick me up on the days when I felt low.

Erik Weihenmayer is simply one of the most remarkable men I have ever met. When Erik was in ninth grade, he lost his ability to see. For many of us, navigating without vision would have restricted our world in a million different ways, but he came to a place where he decided to take "pain into purpose, darkness into light."

I first heard about Erik through my brother, Woody, who travels with an elite pack of mountain climbers and extreme adventurers. In 2013, Erik invited me to speak at his No Barriers annual event in Telluride, Colorado. I joined an amazing roster of speakers and guests, including some injured veterans, and it was clear when Erik spoke that he had a gift.

Erik spoke then, as he writes in this book, about the decision he made that nothing would stop him from achieving his goals. He was determined that his lack of vision not be viewed as a disability, but rather as a different ability. And that is where Erik's story becomes both interesting and inspiring.

Erik was the first blind climber to reach the top of Mount Everest. But Erik didn't stop there. He kept setting goals for himself, moving ever forward, because in his words, he "would rather be punched and knocked flat than to be doomed to a life of quiet acquiescence."

The mark of true heroes is that they would never use that word to describe themselves. And Erik is no different. His many accomplishments have made him famous, but none of that matters to him. "You hang your pictures up on the walls," he wrote, echoing the words of his Everest expedition leader. "You set up your trophies, and it becomes a museum, even worse, a mausoleum."

Erik doesn't climb mountains or break records merely to receive medals and praise. Instead, he operates from a need to prove to himself what he can accomplish and to use his story to help others.

In 2005, Erik cofounded the nonprofit organization No Barriers USA. His goal was to help those who have suffered from mental and physical injuries understand that although there exist plenty of barriers in our lives, there is also a map, a way to navigate these barriers and even obliterate them.

No Barriers USA has grown to include an annual summit, a four-day event that showcases cutting-edge adaptive technologies and provides interactive clinics in an outdoor setting. The summit also offers No Barriers University, featuring inspiring speakers telling life-changing stories. No Barriers Warriors improves the lives of veterans with disabilities through curriculum-based experiences in challenging environments. And No Barriers Youth challenges young people to contribute their absolute best to the world through transformative experiences, classroom tools, and real-world inspiration.

All of the No Barriers USA programs open up new paths, new gates where those who feel defined by life changes can feel no boundaries to accomplishment, and a supportive community of people with shared experiences, visions, and dreams.

One of the incredible attributes of humanity is resilience. We hear a great deal about that term these days, and when you read this book you understand what a critical component it is for life, not just to survive, but also to thrive, as Erik has done.

And while most anyone who has gone through trauma or put his or her family through a traumatic experience would take it all back in a second, part of moving forward is looking for the positive aspects that are borne out of tragedy or the unexpected.

It's meeting and getting to know people like Erik that has taught me the true definition of sacrifice through their actions, examples, and humility.

When you finally close the pages of this book, I guarantee you will feel a little lighter. You will also understand that anything is achievable if you set your mind to it.

No Barriers: A Blind Man's Journey to Kayak the Grand Canyon made me think about myself in new ways. And not only is it a great story and a riveting read, but it will challenge you to look at your own life and your gifts in new ways.

Erik's incredible story and his commitment to be a beacon for others demonstrate how one person can make a difference in the lives of others. For him, there are many more mountains to climb, side by side with those of us who have become not just his admirers, but also his friends.

Winter Solstice

The man looked my friend straight in the eyes and said
"You've been through a lot."
My friend started sobbing
Who has not been "through a lot"?
It is when we recognize it in each other that we know love.
We unite in our endurance
As our minds embrace, our histories mingle
We lean in to share the experience
We lean in to touch one another
And we know we are alike.

—Patrick Foss

THE NO BARRIERS PLEDGE

I pledge to view my life as a relentless quest to become my very
    best self,
To always view the barriers in my life as opportunities to learn,
To find ways to build teams, serve those in need, and do good in
    the world,
To push the boundaries of what is possible,
And prove that what's within me is stronger than what's in my way.

NO BARRIERS

PROLOGUE

I wasn't always completely blind. Even though I couldn't see well from birth, I could still play basketball, ride my bike, and jump off rocks in the woods behind my house. Then, when I was three years old, I was diagnosed with a rare disease called juvenile retinoschisis.

The odds were about the same as winning the lottery. The disease causes hemorrhaging in the eyes and makes the retinas split away over time. I went totally blind just one week before I started my freshman year of high school.

On my first day of high school, I was led into the building by my teacher's aide—not the ideal way to begin freshman year in a sighted school. She guided me from class to class and even to the bathroom. At lunchtime, she led me into the cafeteria, where I sat at a table alone, thinking about everything I had lost. I had been afraid of going blind and seeing only darkness, but I was even more afraid of what I'd miss out on. Now I could hear the other kids around me, their laughter and wisecracks, their horsing around. A food fight broke out, and from all the yelling and screaming I could hear, it sounded like everyone in the room except me was in the thick of it.

The darkness was the easy part. The hard part was realizing I would never be in the food fight. I'd been swept aside, shoved into a dark place, and left alone there. Blindness descended upon me with such force that I thought it would swallow me.

I've heard people say we shouldn't be motivated by fear. Even Yoda said it in my favorite movie series, *Star Wars*: "Fear is the path to the dark side."

But that day in the cafeteria was my first bitter taste of fear. It caught in my throat like bile. It writhed in my gut, intertwining itself through every action, every decision. No matter how I fought it, fear was ever present. It was a tug-of-war, the fear of pushing forward through darkness against barriers I couldn't see, tugging against the fear of sitting quietly and safely in a dark place.

Earlier that summer, right before the last of my eyesight was gone, I was watching TV. I could barely see out of my right eye. To see what was happening, I had to put my face almost against the screen, so close I could feel static electricity crackling on the tip of my nose.

I was watching my favorite show, *That's Incredible!* That night, they were featuring the story of a young Canadian named Terry Fox. He was nineteen years old when he was diagnosed with cancer. They found a tumor in his right leg, and his leg had to be amputated six inches above his knee. While in the hospital recovering, Terry watched children even younger than he was die from their own illnesses.

What Terry chose to do next was the most surprising thing I'd ever seen. After enduring eighteen months of chemotherapy and witnessing so much death and tragedy around him, he should have been reduced. As he surely must have been thinking about his own mortality, he was supposed to retreat, curl into a ball, and protect the precious little he had left. And who would have blamed him if that was what he did? Instead, Terry did the exact opposite. He made the astonishing decision to *run*, and not just for a day, or a week, but from one end of Canada to the other. It was a new marathon every day, for thousands of miles.

I pressed my face against the television, watching Terry hobble mile after mile in what was called his Marathon of Hope. This was before the days of high-tech prosthetics. His clunky, old-fashioned prosthetic leg gave him a herky-jerky gait, as he did an awkward double step, and then a hop on his good left leg as his prosthetic right foot went back and then swung forward again, almost like he was skipping. The look on his face was one of exhaustion mixed with determination. In his eyes, I sensed something I could only describe as a light that seemed the source of his intensity and power.

On day 143—after running an average of twenty-six miles a day for over four months and a total of 3,339 miles through six provinces with crowds cheering him on—Terry was forced to stop. Cancer had invaded his lungs, causing him to cough and gasp for air as he ran. Terry cried as he told the crowd of reporters that he wouldn't be able to finish, but through his tears, he said, "I'll fight. I promise I won't give up."

Terry Fox died seven months after he stopped running. It wasn't fair. He'd only gotten twenty-two years on Earth. But in that short window, he had made a decision to run, and that decision had elevated an entire nation. Instead of shrinking away, Terry had gotten bigger. He had lived more than he had died. Donations to his Marathon of Hope fund poured in and reached $24 million, equal to a dollar for every Canadian citizen.

I knew that my blindness was coming. It was a hard fact, and nothing I did would prevent it. As Terry's story concluded, I knelt with tears pouring down my face. I yearned for that kind of courage, and I dared to hope Terry's light existed in me.

I eventually climbed out of my dark emotional place, with the help of my father, Ed, and the rest of my family. I joined the wrestling team, going from a 0-15 record my first year to becoming team captain my senior year and representing my home state of Connecticut in the National Junior Freestyle Wrestling Championships in Iowa. At sixteen, I also discovered rock climbing at a summer camp. I learned to scan and feel for holds on the rock face, using my hands and feet as my eyes. Through trial and error—by thrashing, groping, and bloodying my knuckles and fingers on the rock—I learned that the beauty of climbing was discovering the clues in the rock face, the nubs, edges, knobs, and pockets I could hang on to and remain on the vertical wall.

When I successfully made it up a difficult climb, I was overwhelmed by the wonderful sensation of being in the mountains: the wind at my back, the brilliant textures in the rock, the intermittent patterns of coolness and heat under my touch. My senses awakened. Every sound, smell, and touch was so vivid, so brilliant, it was almost painful. One hundred feet above the trees with the sun in my face and the wind and elements all around me, I felt an intoxicating freedom and the possibility that the adventure in my life was just beginning.

During high school, tragedy struck a second time. Two years after I lost my vision, I lost my mom in a car accident. I was only a sophomore in high school, and my mom, who'd spent years protecting me, driving me to and from eye doctor appointments, and giving me the inner strength I needed to confront blindness, was gone. How can I explain that pain? If I had gone blind a thousand times, it would not compare to what I felt in losing my mother.

After her death, my father wanted to take my two brothers and me on a trip that would bring us all closer together. In school, I had listened to an audio book about the Spanish conquistadors and the lost city of the Incas, and I suggested Peru. Dad agreed, and we set off for the Inca Trail. The trip, which included a hike to nearly fourteen thousand feet, started a tradition of annual family treks to remote parts of the world and fueled my love of the mountaineering life.

I went on to graduate from high school and then from Boston College, where I got a degree in English and communications. I ended up teaching middle-school English and coaching wrestling at Phoenix Country Day School in Arizona. That's where I met and fell in love with Ellie Reeve. When she learned about my passion for mountains and adventure, she supported me wholeheartedly, and I continued climbing, and my confidence in climbing led to other adventures—skydiving and paragliding, skiing, and ice climbing.

But it was the challenge of big mountain summits that most

intrigued me. Between 1995 and 2000, urged on by the Phoenix climbing community, I trained hard, developed strong teams, and started climbing serious peaks.

In fact, Ellie and I got married at thirteen thousand feet on the Shira Plateau of Mount Kilimanjaro in Tanzania, Africa. Ellie didn't have a wedding dress, so we wrapped her up in Tanzanian fabric we'd been using as a tablecloth!

These expeditions all prepared me for an even greater challenge: Mount Everest. Standing 29,029 feet, it is the tallest mountain in the world. At the time, one hundred and seventy people had died while attempting to climb it. And on May 25, 2001, after climbing through snowstorms and lightning storms, I stood on the summit. No blind man had ever stood there before.

For months my teammates and I had traveled together as one, our lives inseparable. I'd pushed past my known physical limits, learning much about what my body could endure and what my mind could achieve. Climbing experts had doubted us and questioned my abilities. But nineteen of us from our team had made it to the summit. We were the most from a single team to reach the top of the world in a single day.

Needless to say, I was surprised when, before we had even made it back down to base camp, our expedition leader, Pasquale— "PV"—grabbed me by the shoulder and stopped me. I felt him stare into my face for a long time.

"Don't make Everest the greatest thing you ever do," he pronounced, and patted me on the back.

Those words sank into my brain and rattled around. I was taken aback. I had just done something that many critics thought was impossible. They'd said I'd be a liability, that I'd subject myself to horrendous risk, that I'd slow my team down, that I'd draw the whole mountain into a rescue. They'd said a blind person didn't belong on the mountain. The secret was that, at times, I had been one of them, doubting, wondering, and second-guessing myself. I was almost as bad as the naysayers themselves. The difference, however, was that I had managed to shove out some of that clutter, to train hard and move forward step by step, regardless of what my brain was telling me. And so I'd found myself at the summit with my team, standing on an island in the sky the size of a two-car garage.

It sounded like PV was trying to diminish my achievement before I could even fully feel it. What I *could* feel were the cuts all over my hands that had been oozing for the past two months. Above eighteen thousand feet, in the "Death Zone," as they call this part of the mountain, there isn't enough oxygen in the atmosphere for injuries to heal. My hands were so puffy that I could barely get them into my gloves.

Muscles suffer from lack of oxygen at this height, too. My legs felt like rubber bands that had been stretched too many times. Plus, my face was fried from the sun that, on the surface of the glacier, topped over one hundred degrees. My lips and tongue were blistered and swollen from the ferocious sun reflecting off the snow that had burned my open mouth. My cheeks and ears were also raw from the wind and temperatures that fell to thirty degrees below zero.

So I pushed PV's words aside—for a while. I went home, spent the next six months in a constant blur of celebrations, media coverage, and speaking tours. But I realized that *before* I had climbed Mount Everest, people had constantly asked, "What's next?" But now, *after* Everest, not many people asked me that. It was almost as if everyone believed that nothing bigger could be done.

It was at times like these that PV's words came back to me. I knew he was right. There were bigger things to accomplish in my life—on and off mountains.

1

In **2002, I** successfully completed my quest to climb the Seven Summits—the highest mountains on each of the seven continents of the world. It is a feat that has been achieved by only a few hundred mountaineers in history—none of them blind.

Of course I did this because of my love of mountaineering and to prove to myself that I could. But I also hoped that I might inspire others to push through any barriers in their way in order pursue their dreams.

I spent the next few years concentrating on family—among other things, Ellie and I had decided we wanted to adopt a child and were doing research in earnest—and cofounding the No Barriers organization, which included annual conferences we called summits. Then one day, out of the blue, I got a call from a guy named Dave Shurna who ran a travel program for teenagers. Teams of kids would spend a school year learning about an area. They'd study the environment, the animals, plants, rocks, and trees.

They'd study the history and its people, and then, with all the prep complete, they'd be rewarded by traveling to that place and embarking on a big adventure.

Dave told me about his dream to add a program for blind teens to the roster. The group had a new partnership with the National Park Service and Dave was excited to test out a new location: a rafting trip through the Grand Canyon. "We'd just do the first half," he said, "some of the easier rapids, and then hike out of the canyon after a week."

He wanted me to help kick-start the blind teen program and first rafting trip. I was a mountain guy and knew absolutely nothing about rivers. They were mysterious to me, yet intriguing. The Grand Canyon, I learned, is known for over 150 named rapids. And while there's a universal rating system for the difficulty of rapids everywhere else that ranges from Class I to VI, the Grand Canyon rapids have a unique rating scale. Each rapid of the Grand Canyon is rated from 1 to 10, with the 10s being some of the biggest rapids in North America. It was not a typical setting for a blind kids' field trip.

"Sign me up," I said.

Over the next six months, we put the word out through rehabilitation centers and organizations like the National Federation of the Blind, and kids from around the country began signing up. We assembled our team of blind as well as sighted teens and met up in Flagstaff, Arizona.

It was an impressive group of recruits. There was a blind girl from Kansas, the valedictorian of her class; a kid who'd gone blind at six years old from ocular cancer yet had wrestled and been

elected to the student council; another who was on course to com-
pete in the Paralympics as part of a crew team. On the other side
of the spectrum, there were several kids who had hardly been off
the pavement, let alone hiking canyons or rafting white water.

The first morning we spent packing the rafts and going over
safety training. "These aren't life vests," the trip leader, Marieke,
stressed, holding up a personal flotation device (PFD). "They won't
save your life. They only help you float. Find the four clips and pull
the tabs tight. If you swim, a loose PFD could lift up over your face
and actually suffocate you."

Next, the river guides called us over to the rafts lying on the
beach and showed us our various positions. The teens lined up
three on each side in a raft, and we practiced paddling coordination while still on land. The guide called out steering directions
from the back.

"Left paddle!"

I heard paddles clapping together, even on the right side.

"Left back!" This meant for the kids on the left side to paddle
backward while the kids on the right side paddled forward. I heard
more clanging.

"All paddle forward!" Now I heard the loudest crashes of all.

"Let's rearrange the order," I suggested. "Let's have the blind
kids in front. You'll get the brunt of the waves, and it will be more
pressure to get the commands right, but this way, the sighted kids
can watch you and paddle on your rhythm."

When we tried that the banging subsided—a little.

Next they simulated various scenarios, like "high siding," a
situation when a raft hits a rock and gets stuck. All the water

pouring against that rock will flip the raft in the blink of an eye, so everyone is supposed to dive to the downriver side of the boat and redistribute the weight.

"High side!" Marieke yelled repeatedly, and eager bodies pitched across the raft, shoulders colliding and bouncing off each other. It all seemed counterintuitive; it would make more sense to dive away from the rock, not toward it. The river seemed like a foreign land, with a foreign language. Like with mountains, I was learning that a river had its own complex vocabulary to decipher, and it was mysterious and overwhelming to me.

We also simulated an accidental swim, in case a person got thrown out of the raft. Each kid would stand thirty feet away from the raft while another threw the rope bag their way. For the sighted swimmers, the bag could land nearby and they were supposed to swim toward it. But for the blind kids, the rope would actually need to make contact so they'd know where to grab. For the next thirty minutes, bags soared through the air, clocking blind kids in the chests, heads, and groins in a human target practice.

As blind boot camp continued, the kids developed their skill, and then, it was finally time to push off.

2

The action began revving up almost immediately with rapids like Badger and Soap Creek, which were considered warm-ups. The next day we did House Rock, one of the biggies, rated a 7 on the 10 scale. Marieke said it was named for a giant rock that you needed to avoid.

We entered down the tongue as Marieke yelled, "Right paddle . . . and stop! All paddle . . . charge!" and we encountered a terrific energy, like an earthquake. The boat pitched and bucked forward and back, left and right. It was dizzying as we rose up the front side of a colossal wave, everyone paddling like crazy. The blind kids in front were digging in hard, but the angle of the boat was so steep, the front half protruded into the sky, and they only dug at air. Then the boat crested the top, and lurched downward.

"Brace! Brace!" Marieke yelled from the back, and everyone hunkered down, lodging their feet even deeper under the rubber tubes. There was a terrific explosion as the bow hit the trough and stopped momentarily. The force was like a car crash, the stiff rubber boat folding and everyone being thrown forward, submerged in massive amounts of water and foam. It was a miracle that everyone stayed in the boat.

Riding out the tail waves and safe on the other side, we all cheered, raising our paddles in the air and trying to clap them together. A few of us missed, but after eight tries, we all made impact.

As we paddled through the flat sections, Marieke described to us the thick, silty color of the river, the clouds passing, and the canyon walls with their different colors—reds, browns, and blacks, like the layers of a birthday cake—each of the distinct layers representing different geological times throughout history. She said that in the inner gorge, the walls rose up more than a mile high in some places, and at the bottom of the canyon was some of the oldest rock on earth, almost two billion years old. She'd smack her paddle flat against the water so we could hear its rifle crack echoing to the top of the canyon walls. We even pulled the raft over so all of us could run our fingers across this smooth, hard sandstone worn down by the centuries.

She also described our entertaining safety guide, who also happened to be her little brother, Harlan Taney. He glided around us in a hard-shell kayak. His job was to paddle quickly to the action and assist any swimmers. She described him in his tiny kayak, constantly flipping upside down, staying under for what seemed like an impossible amount of time, and emerging upright from the dark water with a giant smile across his face. Crazy thing was that she said he was doing that on purpose—for fun. "I've never seen some-one as comfortable in water as Harlan," she said. "He's been that way ever since I can remember. It's like he's half-human, half-dolphin."

At the bottom of each rapid, we'd pull over in our rafts and she'd describe her brother still upriver, in the middle of the rapid, playing on the biggest, steepest waves. I learned it was called surf-ing. Like ocean waves that roll toward shore, river waves move as well, but some, called "standing waves," recirculate over and over, building up and then collapsing on themselves. A few of the stand-ing waves were giant curlers that were glassy and smooth. Harlan would ride them like a rodeo cowboy on a bucking bronco and use their energy to execute superhuman maneuvers like cartwheels and flips. Even from a long way away and in the midst of the roar of the river, I could hear Harlan whooping with joy as he rode these giant liquid beasts. His kayak was an extension of his body, work-ing with him in perfect sync.

That evening, Harlan gave me a tour of his kayak. The smooth plastic felt like Tupperware, but it was banged up in a few places where he had hit obstacles. It had a blunt point in front and sharp edges on the sides for dipping in and catching waves. I felt the in-side seat and the knee braces he used to steer and the neoprene skirt that he stretched over the opening of the cockpit to stop the water from pouring in when he was upside down. Finally, I felt his paddle, with its straight shaft and wide scooping paddle blades, all impossibly light and constructed from carbon fiber.

"Try it out if you want," he said. We were beached on the edge of a huge calm eddy, which I'd recently learned was a section on the side of a river that recirculated upstream. Sometimes they were flat and calm like this one.

I squeezed into the cockpit. It felt cramped and claustrophobic. Harlan pushed me out into waist-deep water. I tried to paddle, but the kayak was so squirrelly it kept going back and forth, left and right, like an overly sensitive steering wheel. I leaned over to take a next paddle and immediately tipped over, slapping face-first into the cold water. I didn't have Harlan's spray skirt around me and immediately came out of the boat and was swimming. Harlan was right there to grab me and yank me to shore, along with his kayak, now upside down and filled with fifty gallons of water. I shivered.

"It takes a little to get used to," he said gently.

The next morning, Harlan approached me with a question. "We have these inflatable rubber kayaks on the trip. They're called 'duckies.' They're way more forgiving than a hard-shell kayak. They're pretty stable in a rapid. Normally, we let folks paddle them through some of the easy stuff, but I don't have enough experience with blindness to know. Should we let the blind kids paddle them?"

Not being a water person, I didn't have an answer, but I was even more impressed by Harlan. Instead of making a snap judgment one way or the other, he was using this first trip as a laboratory. "Why don't I be the guinea pig?" I said.

I followed his footsteps over to the shore and got a tour of a ducky. It was the same soft, rugged material as a raft and much longer and wider than Harlan's kayak. If his hard-shell was a finely tuned sports car, then this was a tank. We pushed off with Harlan in the water in front of me. He yelled, "How about I blow a whistle and you follow me?"

I paddled furiously and managed to stay behind him, more or less, through the next small riffle. It was exciting to be in my own boat, even if it was a tank versus a Porsche, and it was thrilling and scary being bounced around by the waves that came from all directions and crashed over my boat.

3

Besides experiencing the exciting white water, each day we'd pull the rafts over and hike up incredible side canyons with pools of water and rushing waterfalls that you could stand under and get a shower. All the blind kids were given adjustable hiking poles, and I showed them how to lengthen and shorten them according to how tall each person was. We showed the sighted teens how to guide their blind partners by ringing a bear bell in front of them and calling out guiding instructions.

One night, Marieke sat us in a circle and told us about the first expedition down the Grand Canyon. "It was led by Major John Wesley Powell. Like some of you, he had a disability, too. He'd lost an arm in the Civil War. His dream of exploring this canyon became an obsession. Some of his special wooden boats bashed into the rocks and sank. Many of their provisions washed down the river, lost. They almost starved to death along the way. Imagine, for Powell and his crew . . . they had no idea whether their journey would end in triumph, or whether they'd drop off the face of a massive waterfall and plunge to their deaths."

The next day, we hiked up to an old tunnel dug into the rock. Marieke said the Grand Canyon was almost lost to a giant dam that was planned for construction there, and it would have drowned the canyon. It was pitch black inside the tunnel, the perfect setting to reverse roles. For the next hour, the blind kids led their sighted partners through the winding passage, and the darkness was pierced by the cries of disoriented teenagers who had gone from being guides to being the guided.

Toward the end of the week, the team had graduated to blind and sighted duos paddling on tandem duckies through the small rapids, and then to blind kids paddling solo and following Harlan, and finally to two blind teens paddling together. They'd zig-zag through the waves, getting "window shaded," turned sideways, and dumped out of the boat, with Harlan always right there to tow them back to their duckies and help them back aboard.

I traded off with the kids as well, and one day after an exhilarating rapid, Harlan said, "You're pretty good. You should learn how to paddle a hard-shell kayak, and someday, I'll guide you down the whole canyon."

I thought about the baby rapids I'd just come through in the ducky; they were plenty scary and difficult. We'd all been avoiding even the medium-size ones. The real monsters were all on the second half of the trip, which we were skipping. And, I had tried his kayak in flat water and had lasted less than a minute before tipping over. "Sure" was all I was able to offer weakly in reply.

On the last night, we sat in a circle and talked about the trip's highs and lows. For one of the sighted kids, his highlight was learning to guide his blind partner down the trail. For others it was the thrill of the big rapids. For Chase, one of the blind kids, it was sprinting through Redwall Cavern, a huge beach the size of a couple of football fields, with nothing to trip over.

"What did that feel like?" another kid asked him.

"Well, it felt kind of like I was a bird let out of a cage," Chase replied. "I love running full throttle. I'd never done it before. I have to admit, I don't like falling down, which I do a lot."

He paused for a few seconds and then continued, "I know it sounds stupid, but I think I've figured something out. I want to run more, but I think I'm going to fall a lot. Falling sucks, but that's just part of it. I've got to get up and keep running. I guess what I mean is that you can't run if you're not willing to fall."

The entire group, myself included, sat back speechless. I wasn't sure if Chase's revelation was foolish or one of the wisest things I'd ever heard. I tended to think the latter. What Chase said made me think about Harlan's offer to kayak the entire length of the Grand Canyon. I wondered if it might be possible.

4

Any time my friend Rob Raker stopped by the house, both my son, Arjun, and my daughter, Emma, would grin excitedly, shout out "Uncle Rob!" and run up to greet him. I had first met Rob in Antarctica, where I was climbing Vinson Massif and he was part of a production crew filming a television show. We connected again on another adventuring trip, three years later, and became fast friends both on expeditions around the world and back home in Colorado, where we both lived with our families.

Rob would take Arjun out in the yard to kick the soccer ball around or play catch. Once he showed up with a Red Raptor Osprey Sport Kite, and we all went to the top of a nearby mesa where the wind was gusting hard. He taught Arjun how to play out the kite strings as he ran into the wind, and how to make the kite perform acrobatic moves, climbing and diving and inverting. Often, he'd arrive with little gifts in hand like a feather from a prairie falcon, a chunk of fool's gold, or the vertebrae he'd found of a small animal. He'd have the kids explore the skeleton and make conjectures based on their observations. "Exactly," he'd say when they were onto something.

Rob also loved to go rock climbing, skiing, hiking in the foothills, and whitewater kayaking. I told him that kayaking intrigued me and that I'd taken a class in a pool to learn to roll, but I'd never quite gotten it.

"I can teach you to roll in two hours," Rob declared.

I privately wondered how that would work, but I had learned by now not to doubt this guy. When you flip a hard-shell kayak—either by getting hit by a wave, ramming into a rock, or just by tipping over—you are still sitting in the boat, but you are now upside down underwater. The "roll," simply stated, involves going from being upside down to being right-side up. But being blind, learning how to pull off the move was really difficult. I couldn't just watch a video, memorize the moves, and copy them. It was really hard to visualize the big picture. While underwater, I was disoriented, and everything was confused and backward.

"I think this will be an interesting challenge for both of us," Rob said.

We settled on going to a pond near our cabin at eight thousand feet above sea level, an hour west of Golden, Colorado. Rob and I pulled the kayak from the back of his truck and carried it to the edge of the water. We reviewed the pre-paddling routine, including how to slide into the neoprene spray skirt that would keep water from filling the kayak cockpit once I was upside down. I'd done some paddling in an inflatable kayak, so I understood the basic strokes. I also remembered Marieke describing Harlan's roll to me during the Grand Canyon trip, but the move had seemed foreign and incomprehensible.

"I've been thinking about why you might have struggled to learn to roll before," Rob said as he waded waist-deep into the water beside me, holding the edge of my boat. "Since you can't see to visualize the moves, you need to learn them by feeling them and actually going through the motions. And we are going to keep it simple. The kayak roll can be reduced to three steps once you are upside down: paddle to surface, hip snap, head out last. The head is the last thing to come out of the water."

Rob started out at the bow end of my kayak, his hands placed on both sides, as I rocked the boat side to side, from one edge to the other.

"That's right, even more than that," Rob encouraged me. "It's clear that you don't disco! You're very stiff, Big E. Loosen up."

It felt very tippy, but I noticed I could rock the boat pretty far: right edge, left edge, right edge, left edge. Next, Rob went around and held the side while I leaned over in the opposite direction, until the kayak was tipped perpendicular and my head was actually resting in the water. From this position, he told me to "snap" my hips hard and return to the sitting position with the boat bottom flat against the water. After I repeated this a bunch, Rob had me flip the boat completely over, and I used his steady hands at the surface of the water to grab on to and hip snap back upright.

"Okay," Rob said, finally, handing me my paddle. "It's time to put all the steps together. At first, getting two out of the three will be a victory. Say them to me again."

"Paddle to surface, hip snap, head out last," I repeated, feeling the apprehension building inside me.

"Exactly!" said Rob, slapping me on the back.

He guided my paddle to the setup position, so that my torso was turned to the left and my paddle ran alongside the boat edge. "Good setup," he said.

"Now, this is going to feel disorienting and a bit suffocating, but relax. I'm right here to flip you upright if something goes wrong . . . now, ease over and flip upside down."

Blip. Blurp. I was underwater. It was so icy cold my brain hurt, and, despite inhaling before going over, I felt instantly out of breath. The water pressure crushed in around my face. My eyes bulged. Water hammered up my nostrils. My spray skirt and dry top squeezed tight around my chest and neck, compressing the little oxygen that remained in my lungs. I could hear bubbles floating up toward the surface, and I tried to imagine the orientation of my body and the boat bobbing above me, but it was all inverted and topsy-turvy. I felt Rob's hands guiding my paddle to the surface and tried to snap my hips as my head lifted out of the water, desperately floundering for air. Taking a gasp of air, I heard Rob's voice saying "Head last" as I plunked back over. Then Rob grabbed the boat and turned me right side up. I gasped, shook my head, and blew water out of my nose.

"Let's try it again," Rob said. "Remember, the average human head weighs about ten pounds—it's really heavy, and it acts like an anchor trying to sink back into the water. And Big E, your head is way bigger." He cracked up at his own joke.

We practiced over and over, with Rob helping me up. Each time, the motion made a little more sense to me as Rob peppered me with helpful tips. "Your paddle needs to be at a right angle to your boat as you sweep," and "Your paddle blade needs to be flat against the surface. Otherwise, it'll slice through the water. When you're under, bend your wrists from side to side and see if you can feel when the blade's flat," and "Your hips are a lot more powerful than your arms, so use your core. Don't just muscle it with those biceps."

After a few times, he said excitedly, "That was 90 percent you, Big E."

On my next try, I forced my paddle up, snapped my hips, drove my knees, tucked my head down, and found my kayak slowly tipping up out of the water. The motion then stalled out as the boat hovered on its edge. I thought it was going to flop back over. I dropped my head even more and strained with my hips and abs. The boat inched over a little more and then plunked down. I was sitting upright, happily breathing air, honestly surprised it had worked. By the end, I'd performed four very shaky, yet successful, rolls.

5

In the spring, our neighbors invited my family to go along on a rafting trip down the Green River over the Fourth of July. I immediately asked Rob to come along. I saw it as an opportunity to have a great time with my family and to also practice kayaking with Rob guiding me.

To prepare, Rob and I went to Bear Creek Lake, just fifteen minutes from my house. We paddled around for a while, and Rob suggested I try to paddle in a straight line, keeping the boat going in one direction. The wind pushed against my bow, and I felt the boat turning. I tried to adjust by paddling harder on one side or the other.

"Big E, you're turned around backwards now," Rob shouted, "and paddling in the opposite direction!"

A bit later, "Ah, now you're heading sideways toward the shore . . ." And I felt my hull scraping against gravel and rocks.

"Now you've veered right . . . and now you've done a 180 and you're heading back to shore." More rocks scraping under my boat.

Next, we decided to have me follow Rob as he paddled just ahead, blowing a whistle he had tethered to his neck. I was accustomed to following sound in other sports like skiing and trekking, and I'd experimented with following Harlan's whistle on the Grand Canyon. But even with Rob's whistle and the flat water of Bear Creek Lake, paddling proved difficult, as the kayak turned sharply with each hard stroke, and once it began veering, it was difficult to get it to track in a straight line. We zigzagged around the lake, and I was constantly making adjustments to try to follow Rob, still unable to tell exactly which way I was going.

"We'll continue to hone our system," Rob said, "but the most important skill for whitewater kayaking is having a bomber roll."

"Can we settle for decent?" I asked.

At the put-in to the Gates of Lodore—a forty-four-mile stretch of the Green River—we stood cooling off in knee-deep water and splashing ourselves. It was a hot July and the temperature had broken one hundred degrees. The river guides went through a pre-trip safety talk and showed everyone how to properly put on their PFDs.

We had a pretty big gang—my dad; my brother Eddi and his two oldest children, Edwin and Brooklyn; plus Rob and another family. Rob and I would descend in hard-shell whitewater kayaks, while the rest of the group would ride in rafts. We'd also brought along a couple of duckies like the ones I'd tried out on the Grand Canyon.

The rafts cast off downstream. I could hear the kids' happy

voices chattering excitedly, bouncing off the river's surface. "Bon voyage, brave, strong kayakers!" Ellie yelled as she, too, cast off.

I stood next to my boat on shore, kicked as much sand off my feet as I could, and slid inside. I stretched my neoprene spray skirt down tight over the lip of the cockpit, tightened the strap on my paddling helmet, and followed Rob's voice and the screech of the whistle out into the easy current.

The river felt as calm as a lake, just a mellow flow drifting the boat downstream. Staying close to Rob, I flipped intentionally a few times to practice my roll, popping back up like a cork each time. We cruised along comfortably for a while, with me working to follow Rob as best I could. Sometimes the bow of the boat wouldn't track properly, or I over paddled—and once it started going in a direction, it just kept going. Rob would correct me, saying, "Right, right! You're not actually turning right . . . *more* right!" and eventually I'd straggle back on course. Our boats collided a few times, the hard hollow hulls making a loud, drumlike thump. I slammed into a rock, bounced off, flipped over, and managed to roll up on my second attempt.

I got back on course and followed the whistle. Rob reminded me of the T-rescue, which I could use if I failed to make my roll. From upside down, I was to beat my hands on the hull and then run my hands back and forth along the sides to give him a target. He'd then ease the nose of his boat into the side of mine, and I'd grab his bow and use it to leverage upright. If this failed, I knew to pull my spray skirt, slide out of the boat, and swim. But swimming was a last resort. Your kayak partner had to fish you out of the water and get you to shore, and then chase down your boat, which would be filled with a hundred gallons of water that had to be drained. It was a situation that was unsafe and best to be avoided.

I could feel and hear the terrain ahead narrowing, constricting as sound began to patter off rimrock walls. Also, I felt a cooling temperature change as a shadow slid across me, and I sensed we'd tucked in next to a rock wall.

"We're heading down into the canyon now, with towering walls of red and beige sandstone rising from the river," Rob said. "Oh, and that's Winnie's Rapid up ahead. The first real rapid. There's a big boulder in the middle of the run that we need to stay right of. Try to lock on to the sound of the whistle."

My boat picked up speed. The whistle blasts bounced around—ricocheting off the walls as the water rushed and rumbled under my boat. I paddled hard forward, but the whistling had vanished. Waves poured over the bow and hit me in the chest and face. Water splashed me from the left, then the right. My upper body bobbled as something seemed to grab me from below. I almost went over, but somehow recovered. Which way was I pointing? Maybe to the left? Maybe upriver? I felt alone.

Bolts of panic seized me, but I tried to stay focused and keep paddling. I swung my head around to listen and heard the bleat of a distant whistle behind my right shoulder. I cranked my paddle and began to turn, but the rumble of the rapid was subsiding, and I drifted into calm water. Rob paddled up beside me.

"I lost you!" I yelled. "The whistle was bouncing all over, and then it just got washed out by all the river noise," I said through short breaths.

"Yeah, we got quite separated," Rob called back. "By the time I turned around, I tried yelling, but you couldn't hear me because you'd gotten pulled over into an eddy and spun around. Nice job staying upright."

We floated next to each other, our hulls knocking together.

"Definitely a wake-up call," Rob went on. "You gave your family and the guides a good show. But ahead we've got three pretty straightforward miles of small wave trains, where we can work to improve our system."

"Yeah," I said, "let's not play 'drown the blind guy' in front of my whole family."

6

I was still a little rattled as Rob yelled, "Follow me!"

The wave trains he'd described were continuous gentle rollers, and it was fun bobbing along behind him. I could hear his voice better than the whistle—his voice didn't seem to reflect off the rock walls as much. The water felt solid beneath me, and I craned forward to interpret the rising, cresting, and falling of the waves. There was almost a discernible pattern to them, but they went by so fast that I was merely reacting to the feel and sounds without comprehension.

That evening at the Kolb campsite, the guides prepared dinner, and my family played and hung out at the river's edge. Rob and I sat in folding chairs talking about the day. I couldn't believe how exhausted I felt. I was mentally spent from concentrating and trying to follow directions. My brain actually hurt, and the tension worked through the back of my neck, shoulders, and arms.

We both agreed that our current guiding system needed some

tweaking. "It's really difficult to turn around and look back upstream to see where you are," Rob said, "and what direction you are facing."

"Maybe you need a rearview mirror," I joked.

"Actually, that's a sound idea, in theory," said Rob. "They make small rearview mirrors for bike helmets, but it would never really work, as I'm too jumpy to be able to watch carefully. And it's also really tricky doing the reverse-image calculations.

"Another flaw with our system," he continued, "is that when I detour around a rock or hole, I can't just blow the whistle. That will draw you right into the obstacle, precisely what we need to avoid."

That made sense, since I couldn't see the danger that lay between us, and, in the moment, there was no time for detailed explanations.

"Also," I added, "when you did manage to stay right in front of me so I could hear, our boats rammed into each other a few times, and I almost flipped."

"There must be a better way for me to convey the necessary information to get you safely and confidently down these rapids," said Rob. "Let me think on it."

Rob headed out to photograph birds, and I went over to check out what the family was up to. Eddi had challenged the kids to a rock-skipping competition, after which the kids decided to build a fort on the sand with rocks and driftwood. I sat in the warm sand and listened to their construction project and other pursuits.

Dressed just in swimsuits, the kids became caked with sand and river mud as they played for hours. It was great for them to be away from electronic entertainment, instead using only their imaginations and objects provided by nature. Sticks and deer antlers became swords, and raven feathers their warrior headdresses.

When our flotilla left camp the next morning, I floated along between the lead raft and a caboose raft. Rob and I ducked beneath the water fights that broke out between the different factions. Eddi had brought along an arsenal of high-powered water guns—a Stream Machine, an Aqua Blaster, and his secret weapon, the dreaded Hydro Stik.

Arjun led the charge, followed by Eddi and Edwin. They would paddle their inflatable duckies quietly into position and ambush the girls relaxing on the raft. I loved hearing Emma and Brooklyn shriek as they were drenched with water. That would always begin the water-war games that lasted for hours.

As we all moved easily downriver in the rising heat of the day, I practiced my roll and had the kids count how long I could stay under. Upside down, time tends to speed up as your instincts scream for you to get upright again. My goal was to reach five seconds. On my first try, I popped up and proclaimed, "I did it. Five seconds," and lifted my paddle in the air. Everyone was laughing.

"Dad, try two seconds," Arjun said, smiling. I couldn't help laughing along with them. They were having so much fun at my expense as I stressed out underwater.

"This time, I'm definitely making five seconds," I vowed. I flipped again and made a couple attempts to roll up but, for some reason, couldn't pull it off. Each time my head came partway out of the water, I could hear the kids on the rafts counting, "One, two, three, four, five . . ."

I missed my third attempt and started worrying about my air. I reached my hands out of the water to get a T-rescue from Rob, but I missed his boat as I groped around, and I panicked, quickly reaching for the grab loop and releasing my spray skirt with a hard yank. I swam to the surface, hyperventilating as the kids cracked up even harder than before.

Above Harp Falls, the day's first rapid, Rob slid up next to me. "I have a new plan," he said. "I'll paddle slightly behind and to your side and call out signals 'Left' or 'Right' as needed. When you are headed in the correct direction, I'll say, 'Hold that line.' And I'll make adjustments as the waves and swirling eddies alter your course. How does that sound?"

The idea ran counter to my standard following technique in most other sports, but as there was no manual for blind kayaking—and we were figuring it out on the fly—I agreed to try it.

Nerves clenched my arms and chest as I thought about heading into a jumble of obstacles with no lead sound in front of me to paddle toward, but I could hear Rob right next to me. He seemed to be able to stay close, and that was a comfort.

"Okay, there are just two main rocks to run between," Rob called out. Responding to his calls, I paddled hard into the rapid, feeling spray in my face as my bow plunged and rose on the waves. Even with the rushing noise of the rapid, I could hear Rob's commands, and his voice at the end, "You threaded those rocks!"

For the rest of the day, we continued to tweak the new technique, and I was feeling slightly more confident. Whitewater kayaking was beginning to shift from "terrifying" to "almost fun."

7

After a couple of rapids, Rob suggested he reduce the frequency of his voice commands. For one thing, he was losing his voice yelling constant instructions, but he also thought I should be listening to the river sounds and trying to understand and process the information those sounds provided. It felt like learning a new language, and I strained to notice subtleties: the far-off hush-roar that signaled an upcoming rapid; the slurping sound of eddies pooling above a rock; how the narrowing and widening of canyon walls altered sound and signaled the opening or constricting of the river flow. We settled on Rob only giving me information when needed, allowing me to relax some and navigate on my own.

Rob also tested my awareness of body positioning. "Which way are you pointing?" he asked. "Since it's the afternoon, the sun is to the west. So where do you feel it on your face?"

"On my right cheek," I said, "so I must be traveling south."

"And how far are you from shore?" he asked, and I tried to use the echo off the rock walls or trees to gauge my distance. Sometimes he'd say, "The wind is moving directly up-canyon, so paddle into it. If you feel it trailing to your left or right, you'll know you're off course."

Our system improved steadily. We scouted Triplet Falls, one of the most challenging rapids on the river, and despite Rob telling me about two huge boulders I needed to avoid (known as The Birth Canal) and another nasty rock section called The Sieve, I decided to go for it. With Rob's precise commands, we snaked right through the entire rapid.

At eighteen miles into the Gates of Lodore, the river widened and the skies opened overhead. Near a big buttress called Steamboat Rock, the Yampa River joined the Green, adding considerable flow and creating bigger, toilet-bowl-swirling currents that tried to tip me over. I had to fight hard to keep the nose of my boat going where I wanted it to. But after that, it was mostly easy water, and Rob added a few new commands. "Charge!" called for short, powerful strokes to gain quick speed and was needed to accelerate through small holes. "Stop!" required me to back-paddle with a quick burst of two to three strokes to cease forward progress downstream, an important skill for getting properly set up above a rapid. And "Stop paddling!" meant to let my paddle blade trail in the water and coast along, awaiting instructions.

Rob also started yelling out "Eddy line!" to alert me to upcoming eddies, and on easier flat water, we experimented with him yelling "Follow me!" and then transitioning back to me in the lead as we entered the next rapid. As Rob tucked in behind me, it felt like we were race cars jockeying for position. In this way, we were starting to perform our own fluid river dance, choreographed by Rob's voice and our combined actions.

By midafternoon, we made the Jones Hole campsite, where we hiked up a creek to check out pictographs and petroglyphs left by the Fremont people a thousand years ago. Some designs appeared humanlike. Others were antlered animals and lizards, and the kids loved them. But in the intense July heat, our favorite was a section of Jones Hole Creek called Butt Dam Falls. We took turns standing in the cascading waterfall. Directly above our heads was a perfect butt-size depression in the narrow channel in which you could sit and temporarily block the water flow. Arjun couldn't get enough. He'd sit above us, butt-blocking the stream, tempting his victims to stand below. He'd, of course, promise to hold back the flow, but as soon as we'd take the bait, he'd yell "Cowabunga!" and lift his cheeks, and the cold water would come pouring down over our heads.

After the hike, Rob disappeared on another bird-watching adventure but returned with an excited voice. "I found something you may be interested in, but we have to be quiet and walk softly." Rob refused to reveal anything further.

We all followed him up the beach and through the brush, Emma hushing Arjun several times when his voice got loud. Then Rob stopped and pointed up at the cliff. One at a time, he let the kids look through his binoculars. Seventy-five feet up, in a cleft in the rock, was a nest. Emma described three grayish-white fledgling birds.

"Peregrines," Rob said, smiling, "the fastest animals in the world. During its high-speed dive—called a stoop—the peregrine can reach two hundred miles per hour."

The kids gasped as one of the birds leaped from the nest, flapping its wings awkwardly. The bird plummeted downward, but thirty feet from the ground, it caught a draft of air, leveled off, and then lifted up into the sky.

"He might be flying for the very first time," Rob whispered with awe in his voice.

That night, we sat around the fire. My dad had brought a book that traced the Green River's descent from the Wind River Range in Wyoming, south into Utah, then curving over into Colorado. Eventually, it plunged into Canyonlands National Park, then joined the Colorado River, and eventually raced down through the Grand Canyon. He told the kids that in 1869, on this very river, Major John Wesley Powell and his ragtag band of nine mountain men embarked on their journey into the unknown. He said we were retracing history.

"That makes us explorers, too," Arjun said.

As we sat around the fire, I found myself a little sad the trip was ending the next day. It had been such a blast doing a family adventure that everyone could enjoy together and challenge themselves in their own way. The whole family had tried their hands at paddling the inflatable duckies. At sixty-nine years old, my dad had paddled through one of the rapids and gotten sucked against an overhanging wall. He'd ducked in the nick of time, squeaked under the rock lip, and narrowly avoided a nasty swim. Arjun had especially loved riding through the rapids, with Edwin in the middle and Eddi at the helm. A couple of times, the waves had lifted up the front of the ducky, catapulting little Arjun up and over Eddi's head. In the midst of the rodeo action, Eddi reached out, grabbed him by the PFD, and tossed him back into the boat. While paddling together, both Emma and Ellie had also gone airborne. Emma had swum frantically to the nearest ducky but found herself atop Arjun and Edwin as they dropped and exploded through another series of waves in a tangle of bodies.

The big mountains had kept me away for long stretches of time, but on the river, each night, after the gifts of the day were earned, I got to come home. I'd sit back, surrounded by my loved ones, listening to the stories of waves and whirlpools, tosses and near misses, and the sense of connection felt as deep as the river itself.

That last night, Ellie and I took a walk down the beach together, and I said, "I really like having you here."

"I like being here, too," she replied. "But when you're upside down like that and struggling to get up, it's hard to watch. I want to help you, but I can't. It was like that time I watched Arjun barrel down that hill for the first time on his bike. I have to look away.

"But I want you to know how proud I am of you," she continued. "Today, I watched you just above a rapid. You took a deep breath, then another, and you paddled forward, right into it. I told myself to remember that face, because that's what courage looks like. That's what I want for Emma and Arjun. That's what I want for myself."

"It's a full circle," I said, "because knowing you're nearby, it makes me feel a little braver."

8

If I was going to become a better kayaker, we needed to push it further and attempt some more technical rivers. In kayaking, technical refers to rapids with more rocks and holes to avoid, and a more complicated series of moves to navigate through, all with serious consequences if you don't hit the line. Fortunately for us, the upper Colorado River was a short drive away, and a section called Shoshone was a perfect training ground.

Because Shoshone had more complex maneuvering, it was going to be really hard for Rob to guide me while also trying to pick the best line through all the rocks and holes. So we decided to add another kayaker to the group. We'd enlist different friends to be our "line picker," to paddle out in front and choose the ideal way through. That would enable Rob to concentrate on guiding me, while he simply followed the lead boater. In case I had problems and swam, another kayaker could also be there to retrieve my boat, while Rob towed me back to shore.

The rapids in Shoshone were accurately named and spoke straight to my fears: Pinball Alley, Tombstone, and Man-Eater, to name a few. Listening to the full-throated roar of water pounding relentlessly over rocks, my muscles felt weak and mushy. I forced myself to breathe oxygen into my body, but I still felt like I could suffocate.

As we carried our boats down to the river, I had to consciously will my muscles to fire. Climbing mountains was supposed to have prepared me in some way for all kinds of challenges, but I didn't feel prepared for this. At forty-one, I felt as vulnerable as a child, like I was starting over. My teeth chattered. My hands shook, and I was a little dizzy. My mouth was so dry I could hardly swallow. Rob patted me on the shoulder, assuring me that it was going to be okay.

Pinball Alley was a series of waves between a scattering of exposed rocks you had to zigzag through, with openings only a little wider than the width of a kayak. Despite Rob doing his best to call commands, my kayak would often bounce off one of those rocks, my knuckles scraping and paddle clacking. That would send me careening and ricocheting downriver, desperately bracing to stay upright. In that crazy spin, it was hard to tell which way I was facing, and I'd get totally disoriented. On one run, I slammed into a rock sideways that shook me up and flipped me. I swam out of my boat, and as Rob hauled me to the bank, he shouted, "You blind guys are sure unpredictable! You don't always go in the direction I'm expecting you to!"

Rob was joking, but the underlying point was accurate. Every run, even down the same rapid, felt totally different. If I entered angled ten degrees too far left, or Rob was a second late on a command, or I slightly overturned, it would begin a cascading chain of circumstances that would make the run go from bad to worse. The river had its own energy that surged and ebbed unpredictably, so sometimes Rob would yell "Small left!" and I'd make what I thought was the turn, without knowing the river was actually pulling me farther right. "Left! Hard left!" Rob would shout with increasing urgency as I swept toward one of the many hazards.

Tombstone was another rapid that made me sweat, especially under all my layers of clothing. It featured a sharp, pointed rock in the middle of the river, with a large hole and a bunch of rocks just to its right. The line through there was narrow, requiring you to squeak to the left of the rocks, drop down into the meat of the rapid, and just before smacking into the Tombstone, make a hard right to whoosh by.

The flow down a wild river doesn't move at one consistent pace, so with Rob right behind me, trying to kayak in symmetry with me, it was tricky to begin with. But at Tombstone, I hit the line a little to the right, bounced over a rock, and hit the hole sideways. It stopped me flat and flipped me instantly. I rolled up with just enough time to miss the Tombstone, brushing it with my elbow, but at the next eddy, Rob told me he'd almost T-boned me—or, to put it another way, almost hammered me with the pointed bow of his boat! That could easily break ribs, or worse. So to avoid me, Rob had purposely flipped his own boat, which stopped him in the very same hole.

Floating in an eddy above the last rapid, Man-Eater, Rob said, "Don't be intimidated by the name. As long as we stay center or right, it's pretty straightforward."

"What if I don't?" I asked tentatively.

Rob looked downriver and said, "That's where the name 'Man-Eater' comes in. So just make sure to angle right and you won't have to worry about it."

As we entered the rapid, however, I got pulled too far left and into a circulating eddy. Rob shot by and, within a few seconds, was somewhere downriver.

I was stuck, spinning around, totally disoriented. A moment later, I felt myself dropping backward out of the bottom of the eddy and directly into the Man-Eater. Fortunately for me, the river flow was lower than normal, and the Man-Eater turned out to be a jumble of boulders, some just under the surface and others protruding. I scraped and bounced through them, some-how managing to stay upright. My adrenaline surged, and I was hyperventilating as I finally slammed into a boulder that flipped me instantly. I'd had enough. I pulled my skirt and swam.

As Rob towed me to the shore, he said, "That was impressive, Big E. You managed to ride it through . . . until that very last rock." And later, sitting on the beach together, he said, "This speaks loudly to the fact that we need radios. As the rapids get bigger, it's going to be impossible for me to stay next to you. It's going to get harder to hear. We may be separated by a wall of white water, or you might get pulled into an eddy."

He was right. I was trying to ride an avalanche of water that roared in my ears and blocked out everything else. In the midst of all that, Rob was trying to stay right behind me, yelling at the top of his lungs, and I could only barely hear him. Those commands had to be dead-on, delivered with perfect timing and accuracy, and the other part of the equation: I had to execute his commands flawlessly. Being a foot too far left or right meant the difference between getting hammered or squeaking through, and it would only be getting bigger and louder. So with the memory of Man-Eater lingering in my restless dreams, the search for a radio communication system began.

9

We needed a completely submersible, hands-free system, and while the array of radio choices was dizzying, no one system seemed to offer exactly what we needed.

The next spring, I organized another family trip, this one down Desolation and Gray Canyons on the Green River, an eighty-four-mile section below the Gates of Lodore in Utah. This would give us a chance to test a new radio setup. The river was normally a Class III section, but when we arrived, we found the water was flowing at flood stage—forty-two thousand cubic feet per second (cfs). That meant: superfast. It was a thirty-five-year high, and Rob said, "Get ready for a wild ride."

At the put-in, I slid the walkie-talkie box into a pocket in my PFD. I attached the cables that trailed up to my headset, which wrapped around my forehead with Velcro straps. I adjusted the dangling mike against my mouth and finally pulled my helmet over it all.

As I began paddling, I noticed that this new technology added another layer on top of a sport that, with a tight spray skirt, dry top, and PFD, already felt cumbersome and claustrophobic. Now I had a bulky box jammed into my chest pocket and a series of cables protruding from my PFD, wrapping around my shoulder straps, and connected to an earbud plugging my ear. With my left ear no longer hearing the ambient sound around me, I was now listening to the world in mono, no longer in stereo. Being reduced to one ear made it harder to assess space and distance and respond to the sound cues I was so used to. I felt less connected to the river. But with Rob's voice immediately in my ear, I was now more connected to him, my lifeline, and it gave me confidence.

Rob began his commands as we entered our first rapid. Crammed into my tiny craft, layered in protective gear, and with the new earpiece and a microphone covering my face, I felt kind of like an astronaut blasting off into space, with Rob as my mission control: "Okay, Big E. You're now entering the green tongue. At the bottom, there are some laterals we need to break through . . . now hard left. Fight the spin. Hold that line." His voice was now fast with adrenaline. "Hard right . . . charge, charge, charge!"

Rob could now hang back farther from my boat, which lessened the threat of him T-boning me. Once I got stuck in an eddy, and Rob shot past me, but unlike Shoshone, he pulled over in an eddy a hundred feet down and talked me through. "Small left, small left . . . Now paddle hard . . . You're through the eddy line. Hard left and hold that line."

Despite the advantages, with technology came a higher chance of catastrophic failure. Water could seep into the control panel; a cable could disconnect; a microphone could be clogged with water;

and a battery could die. I had to trust that the radio would work reliably. The pre-radio days had been more black-and-white: I could either hear Rob or I couldn't. But with radios, the worst scenario would be for me to be hurtling down a rapid thinking everything was fine, when, in actuality, Rob was yelling desperate commands that I wasn't hearing and following because I had no clue the radio wasn't working.

On the flat water, I practiced my roll a lot. Radio waves don't work underwater, so I couldn't hear Rob when I was upside down, but as I rolled up, Rob would begin to speak. Most of the time, I'd hear him, but now and then, with no explanation we could determine, I wouldn't hear a thing. When we checked, we'd find the radio had mysteriously shut itself off.

Our new system was a waterproof, voice-activated system, but we continued discovering some problems. First, the wind gusts and water splashes constantly triggered the voice activation. Since it was often activated, I couldn't talk back to Rob. The big waves also knocked our mikes out of place, so Rob's commands became a distant whisper. But worse than that, Rob's first word would kick on the voice activation, and, because of that, it would often miss his first syllable. "Small left" became "—ll left" and "hard right" became "—rd right."

I was always second-guessing his commands, and it began throwing off my rhythm and filling me with anxiety. We also noticed the voice activation had a half-second delay from the time Rob said something to the time it was received in my ear. Half a second seems minuscule, but in a rapid, when the timing of Rob's directions was everything, it felt like an eternity. A few times I was late on a call and found myself bouncing over a submerged rock and flipping in the circulating hole beneath it. My roll was still shaky, and I was still getting panicky underwater. I really wanted to take Rob's advice to keep trying two, three, even four times before I pulled the skirt. But when I was under, I'd try once, maybe twice, and then pull it. I was finding it almost impossible to break my brain's fight-or-flight mechanism, built up over thousands of years of human evolution. Instinct took over, and I was no longer consciously making decisions.

The one rapid we were concerned about was called Joe Hutch Canyon Rapid, which came at mile fifty-five. When we arrived a couple of hundred yards above it, we pulled over river right and went ashore to scout. With the river running this high, it was the loudest white water I'd ever stood next to, and Rob and I had to yell pretty loud to hear each other over the roar. Rob grabbed my hand and pointed my finger at the river. "Definitely big water. Gotta be Class IV. There's a strainer river right, a big hole river center, and a huge wave train river left. We'll want to enter the center tongue, then make a hard right as soon as we pass the big hole to miss the giant wave train. After the wave train there's a large rock wall river left we'll want to stay well clear of . . ."

My ears heard the words, but my brain was shutting off. All of a sudden, this didn't seem like a very good idea. I imagined flipping and getting slammed into the rock wall at the bottom.

I half mumbled to Rob that I might want to skip this one, that this was a family trip, and Ellie probably wouldn't want me to try it, but Rob was already off discussing the safety plan with the raft guides.

A little while later, a hollow pit lodged in my stomach as we floated down toward the overwhelming noise. "Are you ready for this, Big E?" Rob asked over the radio.

"I guess so," I replied, fighting down nausea.

"Okay," his voice crackled, "here we go."

Then I heard silence—utter and complete radio silence. For a moment, I worried something had happened to Rob. My boat started bobbing and rolling in massive entry waves, and I heard Rob's voice from at least a hundred feet behind me, completely unintelligible, but unmistakably back there somewhere.

As I rode the back of a slippery liquid serpent, I tried to rotate my body and raised my paddle over my head in the sign of distress. "Rob, no radios!" I yelled, and it came out like an animal's dying scream. "No radios!"

There was nothing to do but try to point into the massive waves that were crashing over my head. I braced and tried to stay upright, lifting skyward and riding down the other sides. Water exploded all around me, and the pulse of the river drew me forward. I wondered if I were about to crash into the canyon wall or be pulled into a hole.

After what felt like a lifetime, but was probably only a minute, I finally heard his call behind me, and I was relieved. The radio was dead, and Rob had figured it out and hurried down to me, now hollering, "Plan B!"

In kayaking, your first plan often doesn't happen, so Rob always insisted on a plan B. In this instance, it was to shout at the top of his lungs, like the old days.

"Left, hard left! Charge! Charge!" A huge wave pummeled me from the side, and I went over, but I kept it together and popped back up on my second try.

As the waves diminished and the roaring subsided, Rob yelled, "Nice combat roll! You nailed it, Big E!"

I panted hard and collapsed over the front of my boat. Finally, I said, "I'm done with those radios."

10

I hadn't been home long and was still thinking about kayaking and how to solve our radio problem when I got a call from Richard Hogle, the head of product development at Wicab, Inc., a company I'd been working with for a few years. They'd loaned me the newest version of their BrainPort device, and Rich wanted to know how my testing was going. Although it wouldn't help me with my radio search, the BrainPort was a remarkable piece of technology that had far-reaching implications well beyond kayaking. In fact, it seemed more like science fiction than reality. The device, comprised of a digital camera, microprocessor, and tongue display, was allowing me, and other blind people, to "see"—with our tongues. This technology allows me to connect with the world, to be more active, and to achieve the seemingly impossible.

I'd been testing the BrainPort for a number of years and even had the privilege of meeting Dr. Paul Bach-y-Rita, the pioneer responsible for this groundbreaking concept. In 2003, my dad had read an article in a science magazine about Dr. Bach-y-Rita's work, and he reached out to see whether I might be a good candidate to help test the device. A few months later, I met Dr. Bach-y-Rita at the Tactile Communication and Neurorehabilitation Laboratory at the University of Wisconsin at Madison.

"The brain has the capacity to change," Dr. Bach-y-Rita stated. "If one part, or a number of parts, fail, then other parts can adapt and take over. This is called neuroplasticity.

"It's the brain that sees, not the eyes," Dr. Bach-y-Rita said. "If one sense, such as vision, is damaged, we wondered if another sense could take over. Our theory was that we could find another portal to send input to the brain. We called this 'sensory substitution.'"

Earlier in his study, before I had met him, Bach-y-Rita had rigged a dentist's chair with panels holding four hundred small touch sensors that were connected to a camera. What the camera saw was translated to electrical signals that vibrated the chair's sensors. When blind subjects sat in the chair, they were able to translate the vibrating patterns they were feeling on their backs into triangles and squares, letters, and then words.

"When you were a child," the doctor asked excitedly when he described this to me, "did anyone draw on your back? Well, that's what was happening. These subjects were reading with their skin."

Eventually, they were able to detect furniture, telephones, even faces. The visual cortex in the brain was designed to receive information through the eyes, but Dr. Bach-y-Rita had discovered that another sense, the sense of touch, could substitute. He had created a new connection, one that was thought to be broken permanently, showing that the brain could change and adapt to new sensory input.

The BrainPort device I was testing had come a long way from a dentist's chair, but the concept was essentially the same, except now, I would feel the vibrations on my tongue. Dr. Bach-y-Rita discovered the tongue is excellent for sensory stimulation. Its many receptors make it very sensitive, and because it's coated with saliva, it takes well to electrical contact. In normal vision, light hitting the retina provokes electric impulses that the brain translates into images. What the BrainPort does is convert light into electrical impulses that stimulate the tongue instead of the retina.

A "tongue display unit"—a square grid of four hundred tiny electrodes, the whole unit only slightly larger than a postage stamp—connected to a computer monitor on a rolling cart, which in turn was connected to a camera. The camera attached to my forehead with an elastic headband, similar to a headlamp. The tongue display went in my mouth and directed the camera on the table in front of me.

When I first tried it, instantly little electric shocks tickled my tongue, like when I had touched my tongue to a battery as a kid.

"Investigate the table," the researcher working with me urged.

At first the sensations felt random, but then something began to emerge. It vibrated in a round shape. I reached out and felt a tennis ball sitting on the table.

"This time," she continued, "I'm going to roll you the ball. See if you can feel it moving."

A moment later, I felt a little circular vibration starting at the back of my tongue and moving toward the front. As it moved, the circle got progressively larger. I reached out my hand and actually stopped the ball that was rolling toward the edge of the table.

Saying I was blown away would have been an understatement. As a blind person, it had been twenty-five years since I had experienced hand-to-eye coordination. There were ways of compensating, but nothing was as beautiful and fluid as reaching out and plucking an object out of space. In five minutes, the BrainPort had just reestablished that connection, although I guess this was tongue-to-hand coordination.

The newest version of the BrainPort I was now testing at home after the Desolation Canyon river trip was much smaller and more portable. I put on sport sunglasses that housed a small video camera on the nose bridge. That camera acted as "eyes," gathering in visual information. The images got transmitted to a small handheld computer about the size of a cell phone, which translated those visual signals to the tongue display. I sat on my couch, moving my hand around in front of my face, holding one finger up, then two, then all my fingers, and finally moving my hand close up against my face and farther away. When Emma was a baby, Ellie described her doing the same thing: wiggling her fingers and toes and using those familiar appendages as a starting place from which to branch out into the world. I felt like a child as I walked around the house, trying to interpret all the images I was feeling.

"What's that, Dad?" Emma asked as I fiddled with the controller and zoomed the camera out wide. The sensations on my tongue were only in two dimensions, like a line drawing on a piece of paper. As I concentrated, I thought I felt a body and some protruding sticks that might be legs. "Is that Willa?" I asked, popping out the tongue display and kneeling down to touch the furry coat of my guide dog.

Emma and Arjun decided to take me around the house in a game of "Stump Blind Daddy."

One of the objects really confused me. It started with a stick pointing straight up. On top was a tiny blob with a sharp point that danced around in a crazy way. I was reaching out to investigate further when Emma yelled, "Stop! That's the flame of a candle."

"I remember those days when I used to tell you not to reach out toward the hot stove," I said. "Guess now it's my turn."

I next moved into the kitchen and looked down at the counter. The tingling on my tongue became a small circle connected to a rectangular peg. The circle was more defined around the edges.

"Coffee cup?" I asked.

"That's too easy," Emma said. "Now try to grab it." It was hard enough to interpret my surroundings, but it was even harder for my brain to translate the tactile information on my tongue into perspective and dimension. It all took time and practice, like learning a new language, and it was mentally exhausting as I stretched to put the pieces together.

Using the hand controller, I zoomed in and out on the mug, and matched how big it was on my tongue versus where it was in space. I put my hand out until it enveloped the cup. Then I eased my hand down. It landed lightly on top of the handle. I lifted it up and, with a smile, took a sip of Ellie's coffee.

I took the BrainPort to the climbing gym to see if I could use it to find holds on the wall. It was a fun exercise, and afterward, I started getting a bunch of media inquiries asking me to use the device to test it in skiing, kayaking, or rock climbing. But I thought they were missing the point. I didn't need the BrainPort for extreme pursuits. The ways it lent meaning in my life were subtler. When I became blind, two barriers had arisen. Not being able to see anymore had been difficult, but the true deficit was that I'd lost a vital connection to those I loved. I couldn't play a game of rock-paper-scissors with the kids or praise a beautiful picture they'd drawn in school. I couldn't tell Ellie how beautiful she looked in her new outfit or catch a knowing glance from her across the room. Without those connections, my life could sometimes feel lonely and isolating.

So it felt like magic when I could use the BrainPort to share a moment or play a game. I played tic-tac-toe with Emma and used the BrainPort to teach Arjun how to read. I could decipher letters on Arjun's cue cards, and we'd sound out the words together. One day, I used the device to look down and noticed a ball rolling across my tongue, like the first time at the laboratory, but this time, it was Arjun kicking me his soccer ball. I knelt on the wrestling mat like a goalie, stopped the ball, and threw it back again and again.

Later it was back to reading, but as usual, Arjun started horsing around and telling me jokes. I pointed the camera at his head and zoomed in. His face filled the frame of the camera, and I studied his lips moving, shimmering in wavy pulses. I lost track of what he was saying, transfixed by the electrical impulses that were my son's eyes squinting and twinkling, his round cheeks lifting, what I thought were his teeth, and, most remarkable, his curling smile. With each new joke, his head would tilt back. His mouth would spread out, and his entire face would transform. I had forgotten the details of how a laugh seemed to engulf the face as it erupted with joy. I couldn't help but smile, too, and the tongue display flopped out of my mouth. Spit flew everywhere and trailed out in long tendrils of drool. Soon we were both bursting with laughter until tears were rolling down my face.

11

That July, it was time for our fifth No Barriers Summit. This one was just an hour from my home, in Winter Park, Colorado, and it featured all kinds of new technologies: a vehicle with tanklike tracks for paraplegics to access the deep backcountry; a kayak that enabled quadriplegics to paddle; a power-controlled wheelchair that a person with severely limited mobility could operate with his or her tongue; and I showed the newest version of BrainPort.

On the first day, I was introduced to a twenty-five-year-old guy in a wheelchair, Kyle Maynard. I reached out to shake his hand and felt a callused stump at the end of a short, powerful arm that was as hard as a baseball bat. Kyle told me he was born with a rare condition called amniotic band syndrome (ABS). He was a quadruple amputee, his legs ending above the knees and his arms ending above the elbows. Kyle had recently heard about me and No Barriers and wanted to push himself and test his boundaries. "I'd especially like to join your hike in the morning," he said.

For a moment, I was speechless. The hike was up a nearby twelve-thousand-foot peak. We had all kinds of folks signed up—blind people using trekking poles and amputees using high-tech hiking crutches—but I wondered how a guy without arms and legs was going to hike a mountain. Countless times, though, people had asked a similar question of me, so I pushed my doubts away.

"That sounds great," I finally replied. Besides, we are No Barriers, I thought. If this idea was real, we had to find a way, and we didn't have much time. That evening, I assembled a team to figure out how we were going to help him pull this off. Kyle seemed incredibly strong. His buddy Dan told me he was a champion weight lifter, pulling off twenty-three repetitions of 240 pounds to win the GNC's World's Strongest Teen competition. But climbing mountains required moving up steep, jumbled trails, through mud and snow, over giant piles of boulders, and across loose scree slopes. Kyle would essentially have to crawl, moving over the landscape like a crab. We scratched our heads, brainstormed, and schemed.

Finally, we went to our hotel rooms and snagged a bunch of bath towels of different sizes. We went to the front desk and sweet-talked the clerk into letting us have a few rolls of clear packing tape used for mailing Lost & Found items. Last, we found a number of plastic grocery store bags.

The next morning, we took turns pushing Kyle up the steep dirt road in his wheelchair. When the road ended, we wrapped all four of his stumps with bath towels to provide a thick padding. Knowing it was going to be wet and muddy, we covered the bath towels with the plastic grocery bags and then taped everything down tightly, wrap after wrap, until it created a strong armor around his stumps. He hopped down and started crawling. Kyle had been moving through the world for twenty-five years on his arm and leg stumps, and he was surprisingly fast.

For the next ten hours, I hiked right behind Kyle as he scurried upward. Sometimes, he had to drag himself through deep snow with his jeans and shirt getting drenched and cold. When he got to a wall of boulders, he performed a cool acrobatic cartwheel over the jumble, landing on the other side.

Finally, we were standing together on the high, broad expanse that marked the top. Kyle said his jeans were wet and caked with mud and grass. "But it was worth it," he said, his voice beaming. The shopping bags were now ripped, the packing tape shredded. I knelt down and put my arm over his shoulders for a few summit photos. Then we both sat silently, catching our breaths. For Kyle, the view was visual, but for me, I could hear and feel the ground giving way to air and space that seemed to swallow me, spreading out into a massive expanse of sky. It seemed limitless.

Kyle began to tell me about why he had really come to the No Barriers summit. He had a goal. He wanted to climb Mount Kilimanjaro.

"My dad was in the military," Kyle explained, "and I always felt guilty I couldn't serve my country. I was feeling kind of depressed sitting in the airport on a layover when these two servicemen came over and introduced themselves to me. They were MPs who'd both suffered severe burns in Iraq. They told me that as they lay in their hospital beds after being ambushed, they made a suicide pact with each other. But on the day they made that decision, they happened to see me on a TV show. After watching, they decided not to go through with it. I managed to keep it together while I was talking to them, but when I got to my hotel that night, I broke down and cried for hours. I think about those guys almost every day.

"I want to climb Kilimanjaro, the tallest peak in Africa," he said, "to send a message to those guys in the airport, to all our vets, and to kids with disabilities, that regardless of our challenges, no obstacle is too great."

Up on that mountain, standing there with Kyle, listening to him share his goal, I realized that everyone has dreams, and that our dreams are not so different. They start unformed and indistinct but eventually take on shape and clarity. All of a sudden, I could hear Harlan Taney's voice in my head inviting me to paddle the Grand Canyon with him—down 277 miles of rivers that included some of the biggest rapids in North America. Those rapids dwarfed anything I had experienced so far.

I hadn't forgotten my previous river trips. I could remember vividly all the rocks I'd slammed into, the desperate swimming, the inaudible radios. I thought about the panic of being upside down, the fear that seemed to melt my will like wax, and the feeling of being massively overwhelmed by forces more powerful than me.

I recalled that there had been a moment way back when I had made a silent commitment to climb Mount Everest. At first, I didn't tell anyone. I was too scared to say it out loud. Now this dream of the Grand Canyon was starting to rise up within me, much like Kyle's dream must have begun.

I knew I could easily kill the idea of riding the rapids of the Grand Canyon and I would be able to tamp down any feelings of regret and disappointment. But Kyle had reached the summit above

Winter Park and decided to let his dream of Kilimanjaro live and grow. He inspired me to do the same. As daunting as it sounded, despite my many questions without answers, I would commit and then find a way. My dream to kayak the Grand Canyon was now clear. I would just have to make it a reality.

12

Rob and I planned a bunch of local kayaking trips and also tentatively schemed about some big waters outside of the U.S. that we could paddle during the winter months. We were going to kick the kayaking into high gear to give me enough practice, experience, skills, and confidence to be ready for the Grand Canyon.

But then, one day, Rob broke the news to me that he had been diagnosed with prostate cancer. The words buckled me like a gut punch. I had not been prepared for them. Not the guy I referred to as the Adventure Glutton for his unquenchable thirst and insatiable hunger for adventure. At first, I was too floored to say anything.

"Prostate cancer is slow-growing, right?" I finally said. "And you caught it early, right?" I was grasping for positives based on the little I knew about the disease.

"Well, yes and no," Rob clarified. "It can be slow-growing. I had a biopsy done, and prostate cancer is classified by what's called a Gleason score, which rates its aggressiveness, from a low of 2 to a maximum of 10. I had a Gleason score of 9, with nearly all cells they biopsied being cancerous."

My mind was racing, and I didn't really know what to say. But I knew that Rob would by now have weighed all his options carefully, consulted the best medical experts in the field, and constructed a detailed and thorough plan of attack.

"What's next?" I asked.

"Having surgery next month. Then we'll see. Radiation. Possibly chemotherapy. But one step at a time. At any rate, I'll be sidelined for at least a little while, dealing with this and recovering. You might want to consider some other kayaking guides."

My mind was whirling. Right now I wasn't even thinking about paddling a kayak, yet here was Rob, thinking beyond his own predicament to what it might mean for me and my training.

"Whatever you need," I said to Rob. "You know I'm there for ya."

Our hands clenched into one fist.

"I know it, buddy," he said. "I know."

In May 2010, Rob had his prostate and eighteen surrounding lymph nodes in his pelvis removed. Yet nine hours after returning home post-surgery, he called me to announce with pride that he was going climbing.

Rob pushed his recovery, maintaining incredibly high activity levels. But as test reports came back, the news about his health was grim. Not surprisingly, Rob's spirit stayed strong. "My wife says my cancer is an overachiever, just like me!" he laughed.

A little over a year after being diagnosed, in the fall of 2011, Rob was over at the house discussing a possible whitewater guide he'd found through his research. He was really excited, though he was a diminished version of the old Rob. His voice had become hoarse and tired-sounding, and his normally muscular upper body was soft and pudgy from the medications he was taking. He now needed a two-hour nap each day. Still, we'd managed to keep paddling and training intermittently throughout his cancer treatment, which was amazing.

Now here he was, giddy with excitement about a potential training trip. Just recently, he'd decided to quit taking the medication and alter his diet to eliminate all dairy products and animal fat, which he learned could slow the progression of prostate cancer. For Rob, who ate anything and everything in his path like a swarm of locusts, this was particularly challenging and impressive.

"The guy's name is Rocky Contos," Rob said, "and he's probably the most experienced river explorer in all of the Americas. He runs a river conservation organization called SierraRios, created to conserve wild and free-flowing Mexican rivers. And he guides trips down the big, warm-water rivers in Mexico, Guatemala, and Peru. These are effectively the Grand Canyons of Central and South America and perfect winter training for you. The absolute best way to replicate what you'll encounter paddling the Grand Canyon: big water and long, loud rapids with imposing features."

"Sounds like everything I've ever dreamed of," I said. "But how about you? Will you be okay?"

"Just what the doctor ordered," Rob assured me. "A river trip is nonprescription medicine with no side effects."

In January 2012, I was standing next to Rocky Contos on the sodden banks of the raging Usumacinta River, the "Sacred Monkey River," a name with some controversy and blending of Aztec and Mayan origins.

"Sacred Monkey," Rocky said in his distinctively high-pitched, tightly nasal twang, "refers to the howler monkey's sacred status in Mayan culture. And also to this jungle area, with the greatest density of primates in all of Central America."

"Actually, there's a howler in the tree right above your head!" Rob added.

I could hear its raspy growl and the thrashing branches and leaves as the monkey leaped around. I could also hear the rapid-fire motor drive on Rob's camera zinging as he clicked away.

Rocky had agreed to take us down through the heart of the Mayan region, in the Mexican state of Chiapas, a densely jungled and vast rain forest wilderness featuring numerous Class II and III rapids, gigantic waves, sprawling beaches, and major archaeological sites. The Usumacinta, or Usu for short, had earned a reputation as one of the best river trips in the world but also one of the most dangerous. In the 1970s, the Usu had been a favorite winter destination for Grand Canyon guides and river aficionados, but then in the 1980s and '90s, spurred by a simmering Guatemalan civil war and the Zapatista movement in southern Mexico, the banks of the river teemed with armed militants who routinely robbed boaters. Word of the dangers got out, and rather than be held up by machine gun or machete point, tourists stayed away. Rocky tried to explain that the eighty-eight-mile stretch we intended to run, paralleling and partly forming the Mexico-Guatemala border, wasn't nearly as dangerous as it used to be.

"When I ran it solo two years ago, I was, to my knowledge, the first person to paddle it in a decade," he said. "I did end up getting pulled over by armed men," Rocky laughed, "but they were Guatemalan army, not banditos. Guatemalan soldiers actually police the region and help serve as caretakers of all the Mayan ruins along the river."

Rocky represented a peculiar mix of talents. He possessed a Ph.D. in neuroscience but was clearly more at home on a big, wild, remote river than in a laboratory. In the last decade he'd logged more than two hundred first descents down five thousand miles of Mexican rivers. Some of these were through Mexico's rugged and dangerous Copper Canyon region, a notorious haven for drug cartels growing marijuana and trading in opium. But for Rocky, the risk was worth it. He was a true crusader, bent on saving these beautiful free-flowing rivers and keeping them from being dammed for hydroelectric power. Rocky spoke fluent Spanish, had an easy and trustworthy manner with strangers, and a way about him that defused tense situations. He never seemed to get rattled, and he never seemed to rattle others. There was no one more experienced to guide us safely into the jungle.

13

The group I'd organized for this training adventure was not exactly conventional. With us were three guys in their late twenties named Taylor Filasky, Eric Bach, and John Post. They called themselves the Modern Gypsies. I was impressed because they were passionate about international projects for social good. They'd taken their winnings from coming in first on a TV show called *Expedition Impossible* (I knew them well, as my team came in right behind them, in second place) and put it toward projects that raised awareness about the needs of people in developing countries. This included a clean-water project in Ecuador and a partnership with a company creating cleaner-burning stoves to reduce wood consumption and deforestation.

I liked their spirit and their hipster style. The Gypsies loved adventure but had never been on a big whitewater river expedition. So I invited them along, as well as my brother Eddi and another skilled paddler named Chris Weigand to serve as a second guide.

And then there was Rob, low energy, beaten down, overweight, and suffering from bone disease and lung-capacity issues from various medications, but poised with paddle in hand, ready to help guide me.

At the Frontera put-in, Rob snapped last-minute photos of toucans and scarlet macaws, and he described Mexico's largest river. From the beginning, we knew the Usu was going to be big water. It normally ran about forty thousand cfs, larger and faster than anything I had ever encountered. But on our arrival, torrential rains had swelled it to almost three times its normal flow.

The Usu was now running at over one hundred thousand cfs, and almost eight times the normal flow of the Colorado River through the Grand Canyon.

I had flashing memories of our Green River trip when a similar thing had happened. We seemed to have an uncanny knack for arriving at rivers right when they were at record flood levels!

From the moment we got on the river, it was different from any experience I had ever had, like paddling through a real-world Jurassic Park. As we raced along, the slurp and gulp of the enormous hydraulic features sounded alive, like riding the back of a gargantuan, slithering snake disappearing into an endless jungle. The shoreline teemed with the lionlike roars of howler monkeys, the piercing calls of macaws, and the lengthy drum-croak of giant toads.

The first couple of days were devoid of big rapids, but the immense volume of water coursing downstream created challenging river features even Rob hadn't experienced before. Giant phantom boils would surge up randomly and explode a couple of feet higher than the river's surface. The way Rocky described them, the massive energy of the river moving downward wasn't consistent. The water flowing far beneath the surface would get slowed down by boulders or sped up by drop-offs, and it would create different currents that rose up, sometimes colliding with other currents and erupting at the surface like lava from a volcano. It was disconcerting to be paddling downriver and suddenly realize the bow of my boat was pointing uphill in a boiling upheaval. Even more frightening were the enormous, unpredictable whirlpools or, as Rocky called them, vortexes.

Like the boils, the vortexes materialized out of nowhere and moved across the water, but instead of pushing up, these sucked you down. Rob could spot them for me, calling out, "Whirlpool on the left! Hard right! Hard right!" But they arose and then vanished, reappearing some arbitrary distance away. It was impossible for Rob to call out all the appearing, shifting, and reappearing features that gave the river a crazy, chaotic energy, like angry fingers shoving, lifting, spinning, and pulling my boat under.

To increase my stress level, the new radios we were trying out provided no improvement. They were muffled and inconsistent, and often I had to guess what Rob was yelling at me to do. I flipped a bunch of times on the upper section, all the while getting hypertense about what lay ahead. Sometimes, the pitching and bucking would get so overwhelming, I'd ask Chris or Rob to link up in a flotilla. I'd grab their boats and desperately latch on. It was strange that even though I couldn't see, squeezing my eyelids tight somehow helped fight the sense of dizziness.

One afternoon, I got flipped upside down by a boil that rose up right in front of my boat. I tried to hit my roll, but the boil bumped me into a massive whirlpool that spun me around and sucked at my helmet. I worked to get my paddle to the surface, but the vortex yanked the paddle blade downward.

After a couple of feeble attempts, I ran out of air, pulled the skirt, and exited. As the vortex drew me around and around, tugging at my legs, Rob dropped in beside me, and I grabbed the stern of his boat.

"Hang on!" Rob yelled as the spin accelerated in a tightening circle. As we flushed down the world's largest toilet bowl, the whirlpool vanished as quickly as it had appeared. Rob paddled me toward shore. "I thought I'd seen it all," he said, "but being sucked down a ten-foot whirlpool is definitely a new experience. It was so deep, I couldn't see the horizon."

At night at camp, against the chirping backdrop of cicadas, I lay in the sand, trying to calm myself down and recover from the forces of the river. I was just glad to be on stable ground. We built a fire, told stories, and got to know each other. Everyone especially wanted to hear some stories from Rocky, and he told us the improbable way he'd gotten started.

"I bought my first kayak," he said, "after a UC Davis outdoors program trip on the American River. It was before I even had a car. I caught a ride from college to Lake Natoma, bought the boat, a paddle, and a spray skirt, and paddled home to Sacramento—about 120 miles down the American River. I hadn't brought food, but figs and blackberries were in season, so that's all I ate for four days."

"Wow, that's quite a solo journey," Rob said. "How experienced were you at the time?"

Rocky thought for a moment. "It was only my third time in a hard-shell kayak, but I was hooked."

That had been the start of two decades of wild and crazy solo adventures, the last fifteen years of which had been devoted to Mexico and Central America.

"For me," Rocky said, his high voice lilting and gentle against the snap and sputter of the fire, "paddling has always been about adventure. Lots of people love the thrill of the rapids, or going over waterfalls, and sure, I like that aspect, too. But even more, I like being in a kayak on the water because it's the most natural way to travel through a river landscape. Gliding along on the river, at its pace, on its level, and on the river's terms."

I really liked what Rocky was saying. Although scary and intense, the rapids themselves comprised quite a small portion of a river trip. There was much more that made river trips memorable. Spending time with good friends you trust, experiencing amazing places, pushing the boundaries of your abilities, facing down fears. River trips had it all. I also really liked Rocky's careful and inquisitive approach. Rob had told me that Rocky was constantly charting and mapping every drainage, access point, and location where springs flowed for fresh water.

When it was time to turn in, I noticed that Rocky had rolled out a pad nearby but was sleeping right out on the sand, and pretty near the water.

"Aren't you worried about bugs and critters?" I asked him through the jungle night.

"No, I like sleeping out. I mean, there are crocodiles and jaguars around, but they usually don't bother you. And there are also vampire bats," Rocky added calmly.

"What? Really?" I asked, fumbling with the zipper to my tent.

"Yes. They are nocturnal and feed exclusively on blood. They fly out at night to feed and drink about half their body weight in blood. When they reach their prey, which are usually sleeping, they use their razor-sharp teeth to puncture the skin. Most people think they suck blood, but they really lap it up as it oozes out."

I found the zipper and closed the tent door a little quicker than I usually would.

"They have plenty of other mammals around to feed on, so they rarely bother humans," Rocky added as I checked all the inside corners of my tent for holes. Then I settled in for a fitful sleep, filled with images of silent, furry, fanged creatures with huge, wide eyes winging silently through the jet-black night.

14

The next day, we stopped along the river and explored the pre-Columbian Mayan ruins of Yaxchilan and Piedras Negras, which sat on the banks of the Usu and had been inhabited in the seventh century B.C. Yaxchilan had been fairly well excavated, but Piedras Negras was like walking into an Indiana Jones adventure. The plazas, temples, and palaces, all constructed of limestone, had been only partially exposed by archaeologists, while most of this ancient ruin remained choked with thick jungle vines and vegetation.

We climbed the steep rock stairs to the tops of sacred pyramids once used for human ritual sacrifice and touched the carved depictions of ancient rulers. We found a sundial, still faintly visible despite the ravages of time. It was unnerving and exhilarating to explore the remains of this ancient world, shadowed by giant ceiba trees, crumbling back into the jungle, forgotten by the modern world.

Back in our kayaks, not far downstream, we came to an amazing natural wonder called Cascada Busilja. Here, a tributary entered the Usumacinta and announced its arrival with a spectacular fifty-five-foot waterfall.

The force of this cascade shoved us back as we tried paddling over to the bottom. What sounded like a thousand showerheads engulfed my ears and water hammered me in the face. Rob noticed that there were actually two waterfalls, one on top of the other, with a big pool between them.

"From a ways off," he said, "they look like big knuckles, with foamy white spray cascading down over them."

Rocky said the knuckles were a typical feature found in this area called travertine, a buildup of soft minerals deposited in layers by the water and hardened over time. "I don't think anyone has ever kayaked over them," he said, "but I've heard of people jumping off the highest one."

That was all the Gypsies needed to hear. They pulled their boats out and began clambering up to try it out. They took turns flinging themselves into the foaming wash more than fifty feet below.

"That looks too fun." Rob turned to me. "The old guys can't get left out."

But when I scrambled out onto the launching point, I found slippery, wet, and exposed roots hung from space. I questioned the sanity of the leap. The landing zone wasn't that forgiving either. In fact, Rob said I needed to leap out about eight feet to clear some protruding rocks and nail the window of water that spanned about twenty feet. I pointed my trekking pole exactly where I needed to hit, once, twice, and then a third time. I stood for a minute, listening to the crashing waterfall and the open expanse below me.

As I jumped, the thought that this might be a really stupid idea flashed through my mind. Then I was soaring through the air, for longer than I would have expected or intended, my stomach flip-flopping, my arms flailing in windmills, and then my body slapped hard into the roiling pool. As my head emerged, I heard whoops and hollering from the onlookers, but I immediately knew something was wrong. Like a bonehead, I'd left on my helmet, and upon entry, the visor had snapped my head back. My neck felt rubbery, with the tendons firing, like I had been whiplashed.

As I clung to a rock on the side of the pool trying to stretch my neck, Rob leaped. Eddi and the gang described his jump to me. Rob leaned too far backward in the air and hit the water at a bad angle, like he was reclining too far back in a chair. The impact lurched his upper body abruptly forward, and when he reemerged, he flailed and groaned, barely able to swim to shore. The boys immediately swam in and pulled him out, but as he lay on his back in the sun, Rob continued to grimace in pain. Immediately he knew he'd made a big mistake. His medications had weakened his bones, and he feared he'd ruptured a disc or caused a compression fracture in one of his vertebrae.

For the rest of the day, Rob couldn't get comfortable. He couldn't rotate to look from side to side without being in excruciating pain. Sitting in a kayak was out of the question. He took some muscle relaxants and a dose of anti-inflammatory meds, and to his chagrin and disappointment, he was reduced to lying on his back on one of the rafts for the rest of the day.

He did manage to sit up to report, as we pulled in to camp that evening, that a ten-foot-long crocodile was entering the water, slithering away from the exact spot we intended to set up camp. "That should make you want to hit your roll, Big E," he said weakly.

Winning my first high school wrestling tournament at New Milford, CT. *Permission by Weihenmayer Family Collection*

Ellie and I share wedding vows on the Shira Plateau at 12,622 feet on Kilimanjaro. *Courtesy of Jeff Hauser*

After my mother's death, trekking the world's mountains helps my family to heal. (L to R) Eddi, me, Mark, Ed. *Permission by Weihenmayer Family Collection*

Terry Fox on his historic Marathon of Hope across Canada. Terry passes away before he finishes the run, but the movement he began raised almost seven-hundred-million dollars for cancer research. *Permission by CP Images*

With my teammates Jeff Evans (L) and Eric Alexander (R) on the summit of Mount Everest in 2001. *Courtesy of Luis Benzitez*

Our team leader, Pasquale "PV" Scaturro, outside his tent at Camp III on Mount Everest. *Permission by PV Scaturro*

At 16 years old, Erik was the youngest recipient of a guide dog in the state of Connecticut, a German Shepherd named Wizard. *Permission by Weihenmayer Family Collection*

The beautiful Grand Canyon. *Permission by No Barriers USA*

I'm blown away by Harlan Taney, our kayak safety guide, as he surfs the waves of the Grand Canyon like a rodeo cowboy. As his sister, Marieke, describes, "It's like he's half human, half dolphin." *Courtesy of James Q Martin*

Our first photo of Arjun. Ellie says he looks like a poet, about to tell us a secret so profound that it may change our whole world. *Permission by Weihenmayer Family Collection*

Rob Raker (L) on one of his many ascents in Yosemite Valley. *Courtesy of Kevin Steele*

I join Rob, the Adventure Glutton, in a desperate attempt to polish off a pan of spaghetti on one of our many adventures. *Courtesy of Kevin Steele*

Playing "mechanical bull" with Arjun and Emma. The goal is to hang on for a full minute. They never make it to the end, always winding up in a pile, with the mechanical bull snorting over the tangle of bodies. *Courtesy of Ellen Weihenmayer*

Arjun's first birthday party in America with his two best friends, Ryan (L) and Gabe (R). *Courtesy of Ellen Weihenmayer*

We embark on our San Juan River journey. Those early trips give my kids the chance to express their imaginations. Sticks and deer antlers become swords, and raven feathers their warrior head-dresses. *Courtesy of Kathleen Moffett*

The sound of the river echoes off canyon walls during my first kayaking adventure on the Green River's Gates of Lodore. *Courtesy of Rob Raker*

Rob guides me through Split Mountain, a succession of six rapids that mark the end of the Gates of Lodore. *Courtesy of Greg Winstonn*

With the help of BrainPort, I play tic-tac-toe with Emma. *Courtesy of Michael Brown*

Utilizing his first hiking system of bath towels and packing tape, Kyle Maynard crabs to the top of a 12,000-foot peak above Winter Park, CO, during our 2011 No Barriers Summit. *Courtesy of Clyde Soles*

"Robo-Kyle" Maynard ascends Mount Kilimanjaro in 2012, becoming the first quadruple amputee to reach the summit. *Permission by Kyle Maynard and k2 Adventures Foundation*

I liked hearing him joke around, but it was torture to see Rob so reduced. He had been hands down the toughest guy I knew, unbreakable, indestructible, like a superhero. He'd led me up many spectacular rock and ice climbs, patiently taught me to kayak, and rescued me in rivers and dragged me to shore countless times, and here he was, now as imperfect as the rest of us, like Superman having just encountered kryptonite.

That night at camp, everyone pushed Rocky for more stories. The Gypsies, who were on their first big river trip and new to white water, wanted to know if he'd ever had any close calls.

"Well, I've lost my boat while kayaking a couple of times, and I don't recommend that," he said. He went on to tell us about that happening to him once on a remote river in Peru when he had no choice but to try to go through a river-wide hole. He was tossed from his kayak and had to be rescued by his paddling partner who was in the kayak behind him. They were able to recover his boat the following day.

Rob urged Rocky to tell us about the Kern in California and a rapid called the Royal Flush, which is a legit class V/VI that about 99 percent of paddlers will not even attempt to go through. They get out of the water and carry their boats past it. But because Rocky had run it a few times before, he decided to go one more time. But this time, his boat drifted far left and hit a large wall that flipped him over and he had to pull the skirt.

But that was far from the end of the story. Rocky got pushed into an underwater alcove and got stuck there by his PFD. Running out of air, he quickly removed the PFD, but then found himself being swept along by the current still submerged. "I was so oxygen deprived at this point," he recounted, "that I was about to pass out when my head finally popped out of the water after about ninety seconds under. My friends fished me out after I'd swam about a third of a mile and deposited me on shore. I'd lost my paddle, my PFD, and one of my Teva sandals. I lay on a warm rock like a dead lizard for at least a half an hour, reviving and reliving my experience. I realized it was the closest I've ever come to dying."

Everyone was quiet as they contemplated themselves shoved against that undercut. I knew I didn't have the wherewithal to think my way out after thirty seconds of near drowning. Thankfully, Rob broke the dead silence.

"Big E," he said, "as I keep saying, you can hold your breath a lot longer than you think."

"Hope I never have to learn," I said softly.

"Yes," Rocky reminisced in his typical mild-mannered voice. "Good to be able to hold your breath. Where we're going tomorrow, we may need that skill. We're heading into the Gran Cañon de San José. It's about twenty miles through a constricted gorge. It possesses, by far, the largest rapids we've seen, but with this unusual water flow, it will have some serious hydraulic features, including haystacks—big standing waves that break on their upstream face, back on themselves; powerful and shifting eddy lines; and of course, phantom whirlpools, some so big they may hold you under for more than a minute. I won't tell each of you what to do. It's your choice, but if you kayak, some of you will flip and probably swim, and a swim through this canyon will mean a very long one. The vertical walls make it impossible to get to shore, and there's so much water coursing through the canyon, the waves crash against the sidewalls and push you back into the middle of the river."

Rocky's words were followed by an even longer silence than before. I tried to stretch my neck that screamed back at me. And I thought of Rob with a possible fractured spine. This time, I broke the pause. "Rocky, with that lovely description, I think I'm out!"

15

I woke up the next morning groggy and unsettled after a fitful night. The good news was, the day started with some really fun paddling over the waterfalls of the Río Chocolja, a tributary of the Usu. Rob described deep, turquoise-colored water, with tiers of small waterfalls as far as he could see up the canyon. We hiked our boats upstream and ran five of the drops, including one about eight feet high. Rocky had offered to guide me, and he called commands, yelling "Paddle hard!" as I hit the edge, hearing the rush of the water ahead, the open chasm below, and the churning slosh at the bottom. I'd go momentarily airborne, then land nose first, slapping down flat. Sometimes I flipped, but more often I stayed upright. It was momentarily frightening, then exhilarating, then a relief.

Taylor of the Gypsies had a little mishap when he went over the big waterfall at too steep an angle and too far to the right. He bashed the nose of his kayak against an underwater rock, got stuck, and swam out. Afterward, the snout of his boat was totally dented inward.

Eddi in his inflatable ducky was the comic relief. His massive, muscular, 230-pound frame barely fit in his boat, and he came in sideways, hung up on the lip of the drop. He then toppled over sideways with his arms flailing, *kerplunking* into the pool below. When he popped back up to the surface, the yellow ducky came down after him, bonking him on the head.

In the afternoon, we entered the main gorge, and I could hear the limestone walls closing in and soaring thousands of feet straight out of the river.

Rob surprised me when he decided to run it in his kayak, even though he had to remain rigid, unable to twist his torso. He wriggled into his kayak slowly and carefully like a ninety-year-old man. It was no surprise that the Gypsies decided to run it, too. I hopped into the front of a double inflatable ducky with Eddi, not ready to kayak, but still unwilling to miss the action.

Rocky was correct: The power of the water roiling through this constricted canyon sped up the current, intensified the rapids, and magnified the boils, vortexes, and eddy lines. And instead of separated rapids, broken up by calm pools, this stretch seemed to surge and compound into one long, violent maelstrom.

The group carnage began immediately. Taylor flipped a record nine times in the first rapid, La Linea, which Rocky had warned would feel "very Grand Canyon–like: big and fast and hard to stay on line." John fared much worse, however, flipping at the top of La Linea and swimming, emerging, and disappearing as he was carried downriver. As his head appeared, Rob had somehow gotten over to him and yelled "Grab on!" and the two roared down the turbulent gauntlet together, with Rob paddling furiously, looking for any escape to shore.

There was so much volume, however, the waves rose up the sides of the canyon walls, and each time he'd get near the side, the massive waves would collapse over him and shove him back toward the center of the river. The power of the water was so strong, at one point Rob had to yell for John to let go. He was about to flip himself and, with his injury, didn't want to have two swimmers in jeopardy.

As John let go, a massive haystack hit Rob sideways, and he had to test his theory. It knocked him over, but after three tries, he was up again, looking for John's head bobbing somewhere below. It was a shock when he saw John appear, resurfacing some two hundred feet down the canyon, a very long time to be underwater. Rob raced downstream and got to John again, and the two rode the furious energy, Rob using all he had to avoid the huge whirlpools that were materializing all around him.

Out of breath and totally spent, John yelled desperately, "Don't leave me, Rob! I don't have much left! I'm done!" He was gurgling, his mouth getting filled with water. After another two miles, the canyon finally widened a bit, and Rob found some rocks where he deposited John, who lay on his belly, gasping, moaning, and spitting out great gobs of brown water. Finally, John pulled himself up to his knees, then his feet. He wrapped his arms around Rob.

"Not so tight." Rob winced with pain.

"You saved my life," John said, and he sank down again, hanging his head in exhaustion.

While all of this was going on, Eddi and I were having plenty of drama of our own in the double-ducky inflatable. As hard as we paddled, the energy of the river was taking us where it wanted us to go. Several times we rode up one of those crashing waves against the canyon walls, got upended, and spilled into the river with whirlpools forming right below us.

A ducky has a lot of buoyancy, so I latched onto the upside-down handle, while the monstrous spin cycle grabbed my feet. If my shoes hadn't been tied tightly, they would have been sucked right off, and if I hadn't been holding on with all my strength, my body would have been pulled down with them.

When there was finally a break in the action, we took a rest on shore, and I approached Rob, who was sitting quietly on his kayak, taking a drink from his water bottle.

"I heard you finally got some exercise on this trip," I said.

"Exactly, Big E. It was the beginning of my new Gypsy fitness plan. A Gypsy a day keeps the doctor away."

"Even with a little kryptonite," I said, putting my hand gently on his shoulder, "I want you to know, you're still pretty awesome."

"Not exactly sure what that means," he replied quizzically, "but I'll take it as a compliment."

The next morning, I did force myself back into my kayak. Rocky said that three of the largest rapids still lay ahead, and from the moment I started downriver, I felt so nervous, it translated into sluggishness. I couldn't get my muscles to fire, and I felt like I was about to vomit.

The first rapid I encountered was appropriately named Whirlpool, and it took every ounce of skill and fitness I possessed to stay upright in the chaos. Rob was doing his best to call out shifting river features, but he shot past me as I caught the edge of a big vortex. It spun me around as I managed to escape, and I wound up paddling upriver. I had no clue where Rob was through the muffled radios. I swept my hand across the earpiece, shoving it away from my ear. Then I heard Rob faintly calling from far behind me and far to my left. I turned but caught a boil that lifted up my bow and spun me again. Where was Rob? I heard his distant call from my right, and turned around again, trying to paddle through the submerged fingers grabbing at my boat.

Suddenly, I felt an enormous whirlpool gurgle up just behind me. Rob was about a hundred feet in front of me, calling, "Paddle, E! Harder! Harder!"

I could feel the whirlpool as it reeled me backward. I cranked it up, paddling as hard as I ever had. I could actually feel my consciousness beginning to slip away into some kind of primeval instinct for survival. I was hyperventilating, oxygen no longer absorbing into my lungs and blood vessels. I was going anaerobic. My thinking mind was reduced to a sliver, and I had only enough room to be aware of the sound of my ragged breathing, my muscles that felt on fire, and the roar and suck of the swirling cauldron behind me as it hauled me into its mouth.

I could feel the stern of my boat hovering over the hole as I dug and churned with my paddle blades, but to no avail. I honestly can't remember whether the vortex simply vanished, or whether I was able to paddle away, but I somehow broke free, made it through more of the tempest, and busted through a fierce eddy fence, sinking over my boat, safe for a time in the semi-calm pool.

I heaved myself out of my boat and flopped onto a rock, weak and dizzy. I could barely lift my head as I poured sweat and tried to slow my labored breathing. My arms and hands shook uncontrollably. It felt like my nervous system had broken, like a wire that had been frayed and exposed to the elements. I leaned over. Waves of nausea sent me into a series of convulsive dry heaves, and I could taste bitter acid rising in my throat.

Rob sat beside me and tried to convince me to get back in and give it another go, but even if I'd wanted to, I knew I couldn't. No pep talk or motivational speech could get me back in the water. I had gone toe to toe with the river, and it had won, sending me sprawling into the corner battered and bloody. I was done!

I rode in a raft for the next day and a half until the take-out and tried not to bring everyone else down, but emotionally, I was shattered.

Then, when we got to the airport in Villahermosa and back to the world of e-mail, I got the news that Kyle Maynard had made it to the summit of Kilimanjaro. After the summit in Colorado where we first met, I had connected Kyle to an old friend of mine, Kevin Cherilla, who'd been my base camp manager on Mount Everest. Kevin was now running a guide company, K2 Adventures, regularly leading Kilimanjaro climbs. With Kevin's support, Kyle's plans took shape and his hiking technology began evolving. And now, Kyle had successfully climbed 19,340 feet in ten days to reach the top of Mount Kilimanjaro.

Of course, I was thrilled for Kyle. His No Barriers dream had become a reality. It was an amazing accomplishment, and I understood the pain, suffering, and bloody stumps he must have gone through to get there. But although I could envision him at the summit, my own dream had now become unclear, like the wispy jungle haze evaporating over the Usumacinta.

16

Rob wasted no time coming up with our future battle plans. He had figured out, from watching me ski and climb over the years, that I liked to do the same route over and over. "The problem with natural rivers," he said, "is that you can only do each rapid once. Well, there's a place called the U.S. National Whitewater Center. It's in North Carolina, and it may be a very good solution."

I knew the center. It had the world's largest man-made whitewater river and was where Team USA Canoe & Kayak trained for the Olympics. Rob reasoned that because I could practice on a course that never changed, I could learn to relax enough to focus on building my skills. But ever since my scare on the Usumacinta, I'd felt shattered. I'd desperately wanted to rebuild my confidence, but when I thought about getting back into a kayak, it felt like a physical wall lowering down on me.

Still, about two months after getting home from the Usumacinta, I was there, at the Whitewater Center, on the first of several training trips. And I was silently wondering if I could get back into a kayak without being stricken by paralyzing panic.

I was feeling completely overexposed and nervous, like a power line with a frayed wire, crackling and spitting electricity. The puzzling part was that I'd already survived much harder rapids than anything I would encounter here, with much greater consequences.

So why did I feel paralyzed? With all that training under my belt, I hadn't gotten better. Instead I had actually regressed. Maybe part of it was the realization of what I was doing. You start out in high spirits, totally clueless to all the dangers and pitfalls, and one day something happens, and those consequences become terrifyingly clear.

I had assumed that I would find a way to keep pushing forward, at first incrementally, perhaps, but then building until I was rising in a sweeping arc upward, all the way to a dramatic crescendo. But that had been dead wrong. That arc, if it ever existed in the first place, had been severed in the Usu. Maybe it wasn't always linear, I speculated. Maybe progress was more like a giant wave in a big river hole that rises upward and then crashes backward on itself before continuing its run downstream. If the arc was broken and there was no way forward, maybe I had to go backward.

One of the center's kayak instructors, Casey Eichfeld, had agreed to be our second guide. Since he knew the channel better than anyone, he would be my lead caller, while Rob would paddle ahead, assuming the role of safety, in case I swam. Casey was on the national team, currently training for his second Olympics. I took a breath, feeling fortunate to have an Olympic paddler as a guide.

I needed to start by getting my combat roll back. After the Usu, I had lost it, or at least it had become totally unreliable. Sometimes I'd manage to get upright weakly, but other times, I'd get partway up, plop back over, immediately revert into panic mode, and pull my skirt. When that happened, Rob had told me, "You've got to keep trying. Sometimes, it takes three or four tries. You have a lot more oxygen than you think, but you have to get the intellectual part of your brain talking to the primitive part, and the intellectual part needs to rule."

I spent the morning warming up by paddling around the top pool. Seven giant pumps pulled the water from the bottom pool back to the top, and the water surged out through mesh screens. I paddled hard against the force of the jets, like paddling upstream against a powerful current. I practiced my roll and then worked with Casey on the various commands.

After a couple of hours, there was no way to delay any longer.

"Ready to do this thing?" Casey called out.

"I guess so," I called back, and we floated from the calm pool into the channel. A few ripples rolled over my boat. The first rapid was called Entrance Exam. I went through the first wave. I was expecting a warm-up, but it smacked me hard, and I was instantly over. I managed a weak roll, but the wave had shoved me far to the right.

I bobbled sideways over a man-made rock, just inches beneath the surface, and flipped again. That was too much for my nervous system. The intellectual side of my brain didn't even make an appearance, but the primitive side screamed and reacted. I pulled my skirt, coming up sputtering with waves crashing over my head. I tried to take a breath but instead swallowed a huge gulp of chlorinated water. I wound up swimming through four more rapids, finally washing into a giant pool a third of the way down.

Rob was there beside me. "Grab my boat," he called, and he towed me to a small island between the channels. I sat on the edge of the pool for a good forty minutes with my face in my hands. I was shivering under my dry top despite the warm day. In my swim, water had hammered into my ears and down my throat, and I felt dizzy and sick. Palms pressed against my eyes, I was in the Usumacinta again, paddling for my life.

"I know you don't want to hear this," Rob said, "but the best thing right now is to get back in your boat. We'll take a break, and we can chill out for a while, but you've got to get back in."

I wasn't really listening. Entrance Exam, the first rapid, was like a test you had to pass to earn the right to venture downriver to the real rapids below. I had failed the Entrance Exam, and I didn't belong here. All I was thinking was, How do I let Rob down easy, tell him I'm quitting this sport, that it's not for me, even though he's already put so much time and effort into trying to coach me? I just wanted to go home to my wife and kids. I missed them intensely and should have been at Arjun's soccer game rather than flailing and half drowning down a man-made river in North Carolina!

17

I may have been ready to call it quits, but not Rob. He suggested we move off the main course to the "instructional channel" until I built back some confidence.

I forced open a sliver of light in my mind, knowing Rob had done his typical thing, throwing his foot out before the door could slam shut. He was offering me a way to move forward, even though it involved taking yet another step back. So, for the rest of my time at the center on this first trip, I stayed in the instructional channel.

The channel only had three small waves—with easy drops into flat pools—before it flowed back into the main channel, right into the same pool where I'd wound up after my swim. I'd get down to that pool, pull over, and hike my boat up to the top, over and over again.

On my second trip to the Whitewater Center, I graduated from the instructional channel back into the main course, ending in the pool where I'd washed out on my first swim. In three days, I had ten runs, five successful rolls, and two swims.

After the center closed one evening, Rob and I strolled down the side of the channel. Each night, the center turned off the pumps, and all the water drained down to the bottom pool. As we walked, we stopped at each rapid, now so quiet and benign. Rob took my finger and pointed to the concrete features and rubber pylons that created the rapids. They were now totally exposed. Sunset, the first rapid after the middle pool, was created by a steep concrete ramp running into a concave boxy hole. Then came the devious M-Wave. At full flow, it was two lateral waves crashing together in a chaotic pile; if you saw it from above, upstream, it would look like a downriver-facing M. Two gates pinched the flow into a tight narrow tongue. After the gates, the water fanned out and rebounded off underwater structures and came back onto itself. Immediately afterward, Shut Down made a fierce river-wide hole, consisting of another sharp drop-off. The lineup ended with Biscuits and Gravy, formed by a series of underwater structures that twisted the channel left and right into two steep waves coming from different directions. They were a one-two knockout blow before you dropped into the calm bottom pool.

As Rob described the bottom of this man-made river, it struck me what a rare opportunity we had to study the features that created so much energy and turbulence on the surface. On wild rivers, those boulders, drop-offs, and narrow pinches between rocks were covered by rushing water, but now revealed and decoded, they felt a little less menacing.

The next morning, the head of the kayak school talked me into swimming the channel, rather than kayaking it. We put on our

PFDs, and he swam in front of me, looking back and yelling, "Swim right . . . more right! Get your feet up! Here it comes!" As I hit each rapid, I quickly got the knack of holding my breath as it sucked me down and held me under for a few seconds before finally releasing me on the other side. Afterward, we got into a tandem kayak with me in front, and he steered me through the entire course, further bolstering my confidence.

On my third trip to the Whitewater Center, I was finally getting into a rhythm. After Entrance Exam, I'd cut hard right into an eddy and regroup. Then we'd charge out, making the delicate turn downriver. If I didn't turn enough, I'd blast into a narrow eddy on the other side and slam into the wall. Turn too much and I'd crash off another wall and be bounced sideways into a succession of powerful, topsy-turvy waves. In the big pool, I'd eddy out again and take another rest. The biggest and most difficult rapids I would face all loomed below, and finally, I could no longer postpone the inevitable.

"Ready to do this thing?" Casey asked. It was the exact same question he'd asked before I took my disastrous first run at the Whitewater Center. I pulled out into the channel and headed down. Casey had told me about a hose that shot a plume of cold water into the middle of the channel. "If it hits you, you'll know you're lined up right."

I felt the spray hit the top of my helmet just before I entered the first series of waves. Then I crashed into Sunset, which punched me hard, and I went over but managed to roll up immediately. Next up was M-Wave. Casey said that we needed to hit it on the left and use the force of the rapid to bump us slightly to the right and into the main flow. It was a turbulent storm of white water, and I entered at the wrong angle. The force drove me hard to the left into a crazy swirling eddy. It happened so fast; Casey missed it entirely, shot past, and was gone. I spun around and around, getting disoriented and slamming off the jetty below me. I almost flipped but managed to recover. Having no voice commands, I paddled as hard as I could toward the roar of M-Wave, which I figured was upriver. The eddy fence grabbed my bow, spun me around, and slammed me sideways into the next rapid, aptly named Shut Down, which flipped me with what felt like a violent shove. My helmet cracked hard against the shallow concrete bottom. I was trapped in a hole. I pushed my paddle up near the surface, and the recirculating hole shot me upright, but I was instantly over again. I rolled and flipped several more times in quick succession. On my fourth rotation, I felt my veneer of confidence wash away. I pulled my spray skirt and swam.

That evening, Rob and I sat on the edge of the channel, feeling the sun sink lower in the sky.

"You're improving a lot," he said, "but I still sense a hesitation in you. Think about it like skiing. They tell you to lean down the hill, but that seems so counterintuitive, like the last thing you want to do. But skiers know that if you commit and lean down the mountain, your skis will come around into a beautiful turn. Paddling's the same. If you paddle like you're expecting to flip all the time, it makes you timid. You'll feel it in your paddle strokes, in the way you lean, in the way you turn. It's a funny thing, because the more defensive you are, the worse you'll paddle and the more you'll flip. But if you paddle aggressively, you'll charge through those waves."

18

The next morning, I walked out of the changing room and knew something was up. Rob and the head kayak instructor were conspiring in the corner.

"Big E, check out all these boats," Rob started.

He walked me around the storage room and, in typical Rob fashion, had me touch all the different boats sitting on the racks. There were boats of every size and shape, some with sharp noses like the fin of a shark, and some with fat, stubby bows. Some were long and skinny. Others were giant tanks. Some had smooth, round surfaces, and others had sharp angles.

"In all your training, you've only tried one boat," he said.

He was right. I'd bought a boat early on, and I'd grown used to it, bringing it faithfully to the Center on each trip.

"The Whitewater Center is the perfect place to experiment," he continued, "to try a lot of boats and test them out. You know the course at this point, so now you can change small variables and come away with what works best for you."

Rob was pushing as always, and I pushed back. I hadn't even made it down the full course without swimming, and that was with the boat I knew.

"No. I think I'm good," I replied.

Rob continued talking about the upside of trying new boats, but while he talked about the different choices, all I could think about was the downside. Sure. In theory, a new boat might work better, but what if it didn't? What if it was worse? I didn't really like my current boat, but I was a person of systems and repetition.

My pre-kayaking ritual was the same every time. I adjusted my seat to exactly the right tightness, snug enough to allow my knees to bury into the knee braces and my feet to press against the bulkhead, but not tight enough to hold me in if I needed to swim. I'd ratchet my seat to the perfect position. I'd count the plastic ridges on each side to determine whether both sides were even. It had to be eighteen clicks of the ratchet on each side, eighteen ridges on the plastic tabs that I could touch and count.

I knew the rest of the boat, too, even for all its flaws. I knew the flatter bottom made it tippy. It had a bow that sliced into the rapids in a grabby way that often flipped me, even in smaller rapids. I knew all the ways it fell short, and that knowledge had been earned the hard way, through a thousand hours of flipping, swimming, crashing into rocks and gasping for air, and countless mornings spent with my heart exploding out of my chest, trying to choke back the dread that burned in my throat and threatened to send my breakfast spewing back out. It wasn't just a boat. It represented everything I had been working for, everything I had gained up to this point. Now Rob was trying to open yet another door and shove me through it. Behind me was what I knew, but through the door was just more darkness and fear. The intellectual side of my brain told me I couldn't be seriously injured at the Whitewater Center. The worst thing was a swim, resulting in bloody knees and elbows. But, if it didn't work, if it led to disaster, the door through which I needed to go to one day kayak down the Grand Canyon might close, this time for good.

As usual, Rob was relentless. As I kept arguing against it, I knew I was being worn down. Finally, convinced I was outplayed, I gave in. I started with a boat similar to mine and began adding new variables each run. "I think you may like this one," Rob said as I slid into a boat a bit shorter than mine with a fat bow. As I paddled, I found myself riding smoothly through the rapids. The bow had so much volume; I'd bust through the waves and quickly resurface on the other side. Even when I got sideways, the round surface was more forgiving and kept me upright long enough to throw a hard brace. I was feeling more confident as I paddled through rapids that had previously felt violent and explosive. Now I bobbed through them like a cork. I had my first complete run that afternoon—no flips, no swims.

On my future trips to the kayak center, my heavy anxiety about flipping began to lift. I noticed my energy level rising and my focus sharpening. In the middle of the action, I felt my awareness expanding. I started to hear the rapids and comprehend their shapes, to lean in against the waves that tried to shove me back, to anticipate the jarring currents and fight against them. I was rarely flipping these days, but once I came into M-Wave a little crooked, flipped, and was upside down in the heart of the two crashing waves. As my helmet slammed the concrete bottom, I almost reached for the tab on my spray skirt, but I could feel time slowing down. Hang on, I told myself. Hold on a few seconds longer. I lifted my paddle toward the roiling surface and popped up, riding and dropping through the energy beneath my boat.

Casey began teaching me skills like "boof." In Shut Down, Casey would yell "Boof!" and I'd reach my paddle over the trough, grab the backside of the wave, and launch myself up and over. He taught me to charge upstream into a crashing wave, and by leaning just right, surf it left and then back right.

I hated the fact that I wasn't able to hear Casey's commands in the rapids, so we again started experimenting with different radio systems, different headsets, different microphones. I also began to perfect my ferries, an essential river skill, in which I charged out of the eddy, broke through the eddy line, and—at precisely the right upriver angle—used the current to surge across the channel. It was a science to lean in the right direction while the forces of the river grabbed your boat and tried to flip you. At the end of a long day, we busted through Biscuits and Gravy into the bottom pool. Casey gave me a high five.

"You're crushing it," he said, "but you know what the coolest part is? You've got a smile on your face."

19

During our last trip to the Whitewater Center, Rob talked me into going down the Grand Canyon—just on a scouting mission, to check it out. "Grand Canyon rapids are orders of magnitude bigger than anything you've experienced so far," he said. "You could probably just go and do it, but that's a very big leap.

"So why not go down the canyon and kayak a few of the biggies? Then you'll have more confidence and you'll know whether this is realistic or not," he continued. "It'll still be a leap, but it's the most incremental leap you can take to move to the next level."

I thought it was a really good idea. I'd told Rob many times, my goal wasn't just to survive the Grand Canyon. You don't learn much from barely surviving, from squeaking through by the skin of your teeth. I wanted to earn the right to be there, to take everything the river could throw at me, and thrive in that frenzied environment.

So for eleven days, we went down the canyon in a giant

thirty-seven-foot J-rig, two giant inflatable tubes connected by a welded metal frame. Rob said it looked like a pack of hot dogs. The boat had a thirty-horsepower motor, just enough power to thrust its snout in the right direction as it blasted through rapids. The river guides had drawn out a map for Rob with the rapids I might like to try. The boat would motor us through the flat sections, and just as the roar came into range, we'd slither into our kayaks and seal launch off the side tubes, dropping into the white water. I can't say I was excelling, but I was pleasantly surprised that I survived some of the giants.

One of the big tests was Granite. No two rapids are alike. Each has its own distinct character. Some are like riding massive ocean swells so steep they crest, collapse, and crash over you. Some rapids present a massive hole that must be avoided at all costs, and others are a one-two punch and then you're through. But Granite was known for being violent. There was no gentle bobbing through splashy waves with a "Yee-haw!" at the bottom. On the river map the guides had sketched for Rob, one of them had written, "Granite: Erik will flip at least twice and will emerge upside down."

When Rob read me those notes, I felt sick. And, it turns out, they weren't exaggerating. I paddled into Granite and it was like riding the back of a *Tyrannosaurus rex*, mad and foaming with rage. The smooth tongue was deceptive as it led me downward and abruptly spilled me over a huge drop, right into a maelstrom. A succession of lateral waves immediately blasted over me from both sides, striking me like fists. The massive waves crashed against the right wall and smashed back at me. I was punched by waves coming from the left. Then from the right again, and then more lefts. As I furiously hurled my body back and forth, bracing my paddle against the laterals, I was simultaneously diving into deep, gaping holes that, like the mouth of a *T. rex,* grabbed and tried to chew off the bow of my boat.

When I emerged on the other side upright, sucking in air and collapsing my body over the front of my kayak, I was as surprised as I had ever been. When I'd summited Mount Everest, although I knew it was a huge endeavor, I was convinced it was repeatable. Someday, I thought, another blind person will stand up here. It's within the realm of possibility. But below Granite, still shaking with adrenaline, I laughed—and it came out as a snort, with snot and river water spewing from my nose. There wasn't a chance in hell any other blind person would ever subject themselves to the insanity of Granite. I was confident that my goal to be the first blind kayaker down the Grand Canyon was totally safe.

It turned out I was completely wrong.

By the summer of 2012, I felt like I was making an inkling of progress. I'd gotten back on Clear Creek, near my house, and on sections of the Colorado River like Radium and Shoshone. I was even planning a big training trip down the Río Maraûùn at the headwaters of the Amazon. I'd heard that some of the canyon walls there are nearly ten thousand feet high on both sides. It's no wonder it was dubbed the Grand Canyon of South America.

In early September I'd just come off a training trip with my team on Westwater Canyon of the Colorado. My friend Steven Mace pulled out his phone and checked Facebook.

"Erik. You're not going to believe this," he said. "But some other blind guy just kayaked the Grand Canyon—at least that's what this press release says. His name is Lonnie Bedwell, and he's a farmer from Indiana and a retired navy veteran."

At first, I thought it was a joke, but then when Steven didn't laugh, I was flat-out shocked. I couldn't believe it. From the beginning, as I had learned to kayak, slamming into rocks, flipping my boat, and swimming through rapids, I'd end each day with the same pronouncement: "At least I learned something today . . . I learned exactly why there aren't any other blind kayakers in the world."

Even though that statement was a joke, I had built a life around being the first, a trailblazer, and had gotten used to it. In fact, when Rob had once said, "There are seven billion people on earth, and you're the only blind whitewater kayaker," I have to admit, my ego had swelled.

Now, my defense mechanisms kicked into gear: Maybe he could actually see, at least a little bit. He's faking it. Maybe he'd gotten in a raft for part of the descent. Maybe he had skipped some of the big ones like Crystal and Lava Falls. There had to be an explanation other than a blind farmer from Indiana had just scooped me.

Part of me wanted to be happy for this Lonnie guy. It wasn't all about being first, I thought. This was a sign that blind people were coming on strong, breaking through barriers, surpassing expectations, even my own accomplishments. It was a good thing for the world, I told myself, but close up, it still stung. I had already received a lot of media attention surrounding my kayaking, and I had also gotten some new kayaking sponsors. I felt deflated and a little embarrassed. All the endless hours of training and bleeding may have been for nothing.

I thought about all the massive preparation it had taken to get ready for this kayaking project: multiple trips to the Green River, the Usumacinta in Mexico, the U.S. National Whitewater Center, and hundreds of hours training on my local rivers. It had taken everything I had to keep going. Who is this other blind kayaker here to ruin my outing? I asked silently. But an idea was beginning to brew, and as it got stronger, I could feel energy and motivation returning to my body. When I get home, I thought, maybe I'll give this guy, this Lonnie Bedwell from Indiana, a call.

20

I did call Lonnie Bedwell. I congratulated him on his successful trip and asked if he'd like to meet that spring at the U.S. National Whitewater Center. Lonnie was game and agreed right away. When Rob and I arrived, Lonnie and his kayaking partner were waiting in front of the gear room. I heard Lonnie's country accent, with the little hint of a joke that was always present in his crackly voice. We'd been together just a couple of minutes when he asked, "Erik, what's the scariest thing you can do to a blind person?"

"Put them in a kayak in the middle of white water?" I immediately answered.

"No. That's second." He laughed. "The scariest thing is when someone puts a plunger in the toilet without telling you," he answered, bursting into his raspy cackle.

Over the next few days, Lonnie and I took runs down the channel, and I noticed how different our kayaking styles were. Lonnie wasn't a high-tech guy. He told me he didn't even have a cell phone.

He didn't use radios for kayaking, but instead preferred one guide right in front of him yelling at the top of his lungs, "On me! On me!" He had another kayaker just behind him yelling micro-commands like "Small left! Small right!" If Lonnie was off-line, his front guide borrowed military language to yell, "Gun sights on me!" Lonnie told me his front guide gave him more confidence to go out into the rapids, to have a sound to track.

Rob said our general paddling styles were very different as well. While I was methodical, measured, even cautious sometimes, Lonnie's style was frenzied. He took three paddle strokes for every one of mine, and he hardly ever hesitated, hunched forward like a water strider skittering over the surface. Both techniques seemed to work equally well, but they also seemed to reflect our starkly different personalities.

Despite our differences, Lonnie and I shared one major attribute that connected our lives like glue. "I don't know about you," Lonnie said, "but I can't even describe it sometimes. They're telling you what to do, but trying to get through, just with that sound and trying to read the river by feel, I get so turned around, I hardly know which way is up or down."

I knew exactly what he was saying. Kayaking blind was like riding an avalanche of moving water that shifted violently from second to second, tossing you in every direction. Trying to survive in that tumultuous environment guided only by the faint sound of a voice, by the roar of the river, and by what I could feel under my boat, felt like sensory overload. It was the art of embracing chaos—and hands down the scariest thing I'd ever done.

But Lonnie seemed fearless. He grinned through the toughest rapids and even wanted to be guided *into* the middle of a huge hole.

"Why would you ever want to do that?" I asked him.

"So I could figure out how to get out of it," he explained like he was talking to a simpleton.

Over our lunch break, Lonnie talked about chainsawing trees and mowing his own pasture on his family's farm in Dugger, Indiana, all without the benefit of sighted assistance. "I'm out there with my mower most every day," he said, "mowing around my pond."

"How can you tell where you are in relation to the pond?" I asked.

"Oh, it's easy to tell," he replied, "when you hit the water. Mowing's nothing. After that, I started trying to figure out how to drive nails with my hammer. Hitting the nail wasn't a problem, but it was most often the nail at the end of my thumb. Once I figured that out, it led into building houses. I've helped build about thirty now: everything from framing to sheeting to wiring. I tell people, 'I'm your man—if you don't care if your lights turn on.' My favorite, though, is roofing."

"A blind guy kayaking is one thing," Rob piped in, "but a blind guy on a roof?"

"Yeah, people always question that," Lonnie replied. "They ask, 'What are you doing on that roof?' and I answer, 'I'm on a roof? How in blazes did I get up here?'"

"I don't think I know how you lost your sight," Rob said.

Lonnie took a deep breath and then said, "My best friend shot me in the face with a twelve gauge. We were turkey hunting in thick bushes, and something moved above me. My friend just whirled around and shot me from nine paces away. I still have lead shot pellets in my face that you can feel under my skin."

Lonnie took my hand, and he had me feel a bead just under his eye that I could make roll around under his skin.

"Now, I'm not saying I don't have bad days," he went on, "but I practice what I used to preach to my daughters when I tucked them in at night. 'When you wake up in the morning,' I'd say, 'when your feet hit the floor, if you decide right then it's going to be a good day, 99 percent of the time, it will be.'

"And on the rare occasion sometimes when there might be something come up to change that, I would take them back to their bedroom and ask, 'Which side of the bed did you get out on?' I'd make them tell me, and I'd say, 'Now get back in bed and get out again on the other side.' It'd always make them laugh. That's the mind-set I try to live by."

Pre-Lonnie, I had been the only blind kayaker, and being first had fed my sense of importance, my pride and ego; but now, I had to admit, there was another feeling washing over me, and it felt good. Of course, it was fun to compare our different approaches as well as the experiences that united us, but there was something even deeper going on. I'd read about an old tortoise who lived on the Galapagos Islands in a pen all by himself. He was the last of his species. Appropriately, they'd named him Lonesome George. As empathetic as Rob and my other guides were, they could never totally relate to what it was like to kayak blind, to the shock of being knocked over by a wave that you had no clue was coming, no time even to take a breath, or the uncertainty of rolling up again and not knowing what direction you were facing, and whether you were about to be clobbered again. And when it came right down to it, there was just one blind guy, alone and scared, pinned upside down against a rock, being washing-machined in a hole fighting for a breath.

During all my training, I had an inkling how that tortoise may have felt. But now, I had a partner to share experiences with, to flail and bleed with. It was comforting and made me feel a little bolder—like what we were trying to do wasn't so insane after all.

It was time for me to bring up something I'd wanted to discuss with Lonnie all night. "As you know," I began, "in a little more than a year, I have plans to kayak the Grand Canyon. If one blind guy paddles it alone, people can easily write it off as some kind of anomaly, but if two blind guys paddled it together, then the story gets bigger, and it becomes more about what's possible for everyone. It says that all of us can push forward and be that inspiration. So what I'm getting at is, will you join me on my expedition?"

"Partner," he said, "I'd be honored."

Rob and I emerge from the depths of the Gran Cañon de San José on my second training trip to the Usumacinta in southern Mexico. We camp that night on the beach, just above Whirlpool Rapid, where the year before, I'd come close to quitting kayaking forever. *Courtesy of Skyler Williams*

I run one of the many travertine waterfalls on the Rio Chocolja, a tributary of the Usumacinta; it's momentarily frightening as I hit the edge and go airborne. *Courtesy of Rocky Contos*

Casey Eichfeld guides me as I punch through "Entrance Exam," the first rapid on the wilderness channel at the U.S. National Whitewater Center. On my first attempt, I fail the exam. *Courtesy of Sarah Anderson*

(Front to back) Me, Casey Eichfeld, and Rob Raker ride the conveyor belt at the U.S. National Whitewater Center that ferries you from the bottom of the channel and deposits you back into the upper pool for another run. *Courtesy of Skyler Williams*

Lonnie Bedwell breaks the mold. A farmer from Indiana becomes a world-class kayaker. *Courtesy of James Q Martin*

Rob guiding me through Tombstone Rapid on the Shoshone section of the Colorado River. Narrow, rocky rivers are a nightmare for blind kayakers. *Courtesy of Skyler Williams*

The amazing Mandy Harvey performs "It's a Wonderful World" on stage at the No Barriers Summit. *Permission by No Barriers USA*

My team and I take Arjun kayaking down the Upper Colorado a week before I leave the Grand Canyon. I emerge at the bottom of the rapids frazzled and breathing hard, while Arjun rides the waves with a dancer's grace and comes out smiling. *Courtesy of Michael Brown*

My team approaches Navajo Bridge on the Grand Canyon, signifying the beginning of our No Barriers expedition. Only 277 miles to go! *Courtesy of James Q Martin*

I learn a lot about rivers and life while paddling with Harlan Taney. *Courtesy of James Q Martin*

I charge into 24 Mile Rapid. Seconds later, I'm upside down. *Courtesy of James Q Martin*

Baffled by the radios' inconsistencies, Steven Mace, Skyler Williams, and I painstakingly test different configurations. *Courtesy of James Q Martin*

Horn Creek Rapid features the steepest drop in the Grand Canyon. Anticipating this rapid over breakfast, my eggs were about to turn into a vomit omelet. *Courtesy of James Q Martin*

After many days being drenched in silty water and sand-blasted at beach camps, it's refreshing to jump into the clear, fresh water of Elves Chasm. *Courtesy of James Q Martin*

After making it through the inner gorge, Harlan and I celebrate. Acoustics are amazing in the Grand Canyon. *Courtesy of James Q Martin*

Harlan talks me through "the line" on Lava Falls, the most feared rapid in the Grand Canyon. *Courtesy of James Q Martin*

"My guide, Harlan Taney, and I test our Neptune Communication system above Lava Falls in the Grand Canyon. *Courtesy of James Q Martin*

Harlan holds his broken paddle as I grasp for my kayak, just below the "Cheese Grater" rock on Lava Falls. Rob Raker looks on. *Courtesy of James Q Martin*

Washed up on the shore and shattered after my first attempt of Lava Falls. *Courtesy of Michael Brown*

Although I'm terrified going into the V-Wave, I silently repeat our familiar mantra: "Relax. Breathe. Be at peace with the River." *Courtesy of James Q Martin*

Going through the massive Kahuna waves backwards in Lava is not part of the plan. Moments later, that same wave snaps Harlan's carbon fiber paddle in half. *Courtesy of James Q Martin*

Wordlessly, we bushwhack through the tamarisk scrub. As Timmy says, "It's time for a little bit of Lava 2.0." *Courtesy of James Q Martin*

I give thanks to Harlan and the river. *Courtesy of Andy Maser*

Lonnie and I perform a blind paddle high-five as we drift the final few hundred yards to the take-out at Pearce Ferry, the end of our journey. *Courtesy of James Q Martin*

21

Rob and I had just finished a training session paddling Clear Creek. We were sitting on the back of his tailgate taking off our wet gear when Rob said, "By next year, by the time of our trip, I just don't know what my health situation will be. So I've been thinking, you should reach out to some other kayakers. What about that guy you mentioned from your first Grand Canyon trip with the blind kids?"

Rob was referring to Harlan Taney, the young kayak safety guide, described by his sister as "half-human, half-dolphin."

"You said he was pretty awesome, and he knows the Grand Canyon better than anyone, so let's test him out," Rob said.

Rob was right. When I'd met Harlan, he could describe all 165 rapids down there with his eyes closed, and he knew all the best lines through, which changed in the myriad of different water levels.

"Where should we test him?" I asked, fearing I was stepping into something I might regret.

"Well, that brings us to the second idea I've been pondering. We need a river we can train on this winter, and I think we should go back to the Usumacinta."

My gut lurched a little, and my face must have twitched, because Rob jumped in. "I know you got in a little over your head," he said, "but you're a way different paddler from what you were a year ago. It's a big Grand Canyon–style river, and you already know it and what to expect."

"I think that's the problem," I replied. "Do you really think it will be different?"

"One hundred percent!" he answered.

So in March 2013, I once again sat in my kayak on the fertile banks of the Usumacinta with the buzzing whine of insects swarming around my head and the growl of howler monkeys above.

Rob guided me through the flat water, coaching Harlan on our technique and systematically handing over the guiding reins. Harlan was observant and a quick study; by the end of the day, we were getting calibrated. That night, sitting together at dinner, since Harlan was the newbie, we tried to coax some stories out of him.

Harlan seemed a bit reluctant at first, but soon he had warmed up and was rolling on the wild tale of his recent attempt to break the speed record for kayaking down the Grand Canyon.

"I've always been infatuated by water," he started, "how it flows, by its energy and power. When I was just starting out as a Grand Canyon guide, I used to look out at the water from the beach as it rushed by and think, we've stopped for the night, but the river never stops. It just keeps moving."

As he spoke, I got a sense he was reliving that scene in his mind, seeing the moon's reflection off the rippling water. "I didn't care so much about breaking records," he said. "I was more interested in experiencing the Grand Canyon the way the river saw it, to ride the flow, almost like current. Fourteen years after that seed was planted, I felt ready, and it all came together: the goal of kayaking the entire length, 277 miles nonstop and alone. I launched at midnight, right on the peak of a forty-five-thousand-cfs flood stage."

Harlan had paddled through the night, everything going smoothly, on pace to crush the speed record that had been set way back in 1983. However, just below Grapevine Rapid at mile eighty-two, a giant boil slammed him into the canyon wall and trapped him there, stuck between the boil and the rock. It flipped him and pounded his boat for a long time. After several roll attempts, he pulled his skirt and wound up swimming three miles downriver before he could retrieve his boat and kick to shore. "I drained about three gallons of water out of each pant leg in my dry suit," he said. "I was so pumped full of adrenaline, I got back in and paddled down to Phantom Ranch where I had a food cache."

Refilling his water jug at the spigot, he noticed his hand was bright purple. "It kind of stopped working," Harlan said. "It was seizing up, and I couldn't rotate it or hold my paddle very well."

So, knowing he was only a third of the way, he made the painful decision to abort his attempt. He shouldered his one hundred-pound, eighteen-foot-long kayak and hiked 4,500 feet out of the canyon.

The next morning, I retraced our journey of the previous year. This time, I kayaked through the inner gorge, the same roiling canyon where the Gypsies had swum and where Gypsy John had almost lost his life. And I paddled through Whirlpool Rapid, where I'd had my meltdown.

On our last night, we sat around the campfire, eating long silvery fish caught with spearguns made by the locals. Harlan seemed quiet and peaceful most of the time, happy to listen to the river stories, laugh at the jokes, and strum the guitar he'd picked up in a local market. But besides the recounting of his speed run, I realized, after our first Grand Canyon trip and a week of him guiding me, I still knew practically nothing about his life. That night, after the others had gone to bed, we stayed up talking, and I peppered him with questions.

Harlan described growing up in Flagstaff, Arizona, before it became a yuppie tourist destination, full of coffee shops and yoga studios. His father, Guerin Taney, had made a living as a blacksmith, but his true passion was working with metal, fashioning pieces like a deer's head out of an old car bumper or an abstract design made with coat hangers and fire pokers, all fused and twisted together. "He was very talented," Harlan said, "but it always remained a hobby. He didn't have the business savvy to show his work or sell anything."

Harlan's family didn't own much. Their prized possessions were three old beater vehicles: a pickup truck, a Volkswagen Bug, and an old school bus. "Except," Harlan said, "we only had one engine between all of them. It actually hung from chains in our living room." His dad would switch the engine from one to the other, depending on the activities: in the truck if he was going to shoe horses or do some forging, in the Bug for a trip out to Lake Powell, or in the bus if they were heading up into the San Francisco Peaks. They'd spend a lot of weekends up in the mountains picking mushrooms, watching the aspens turn to gold, and shooting an old black powder rifle. Harlan said, back then, all the mountain roads were dirt, and there was not a soul around for miles.

When Harlan was nine, his mom took him out of fourth grade for eighteen days on his first rafting trip down the Grand Canyon. "It was as poorly organized as a trip could be," Harlan said, but out of his 160 subsequent trips, it was still his most vivid. He said, "It was like my eyes were opened."

On our last day of the Usu, Harlan guided me through the biggest rapid, San José. As we rode the shifting, bucking line through the minefield of boils and whirlpools, Harlan's voice had a calming effect. Through his commands, both his competence and confidence were loud and clear, but it was never bravado. Instead, it felt like a deeply learned appreciation of the river, a Zen-like acceptance. When we reached our take-out in Boca del Cerro, I'd paddled every mile.

"Rob, you were right," I said as we dragged our boats up the bank. "It felt like a different river this time."

"Of course," Rob replied, "the water level was lower this year, but it wasn't just the river that changed. I'm proud of you."

22

When we got back home, we brought on board three additional guides for our upcoming Grand Canyon adventure. Steven Mace was twenty-five years old and had established himself as an expert river man, both as a rafting guide and formidable kayaker. We also enlisted Timmy O'Neill, who was not only a climbing legend, but had been paddling a kayak since he was nine years old with his father. He had a reputation of being a wild man who did stand-up comedy and made underground climbing films about "buildering," free-soloing the sides of buildings and even tall bridges throughout New York City. However, behind the popular image was a meticulous planner and brilliant strategist. We also recruited Skyler Williams, my right-hand man at my speaking career in Golden. Skyler had started kayaking to be able to help with my learning process and had come along on some of the training trips, and he was such a strong athlete and quick learner that he was soon a vital part of our kayaking team.

At this point in my training, it came down to one crucial objective. We had to become a cohesive team that understood how to fluidly step in and out of different roles and respond seamlessly to the wide array of challenges we'd encounter on the Grand Canyon. The way to achieve this was to log a lot of river miles together. So we all began heading out to local paddling areas like Shoshone and the Upper Colorado.

Over the next year, we also made several training trips to Peru. With warm water, hot sun, and massive snowmelt off the Andes, it was an ideal boating destination, with exotic-sounding rivers like the Maraûùn, the Apurimac, the Yanatile, and the Urubamba. We also headed north of the U.S. border to the Ottawa River.

In 2014, with the trip to the Grand Canyon fast approaching, I planned a father-son adventure for Arjun and me. As I'd been upping my kayaking skills, Arjun had been joining me on Bear Creek Lake and Clear Creek. He was such a natural; by age nine he had a solid roll and by age ten he had a "hand roll," a roll without a paddle. The time was right, I thought, for his first kayaking trip down a big river.

We headed to the Upper Colorado with the team. Arjun loved being one of the boys, squeezed into the backseat of Skyler's truck, trading insults, burping, getting noogies from Steven, and listening to us break out our old jokes.

Through the rapids, his paddling technique and balance actually surpassed mine. I'd emerge from the bottom breathing hard and frazzled, while Arjun rode the waves with a ballet dancer's grace and came out smiling.

"Dad," he said, "that wasn't so hard."

The day proceeded with splash fights and chases, purposely

trying to flip each other. Steven finally got Arjun with a classic river joke: "Hey, I think you have a rip in your dry top." Steven pointed to Arjun's armpit area, and when Arjun lifted his arm to check, Steven pushed his elbow, sending him over. Arjun came up sputtering, and he was officially initiated. Although he was utterly exhausted by the end, he paddled all fifteen miles. At the end of the day, we sat relaxing together at the edge of the river, and I thought it was the moment to break away from the "bro" atmosphere.

"AJ," I said, "you know I'm off in about a week. I want you to be a good boy while I'm away."

Arjun sat still, not that comfortable with direct statements or overt emotion, but nevertheless, I put my arm around him and rubbed his back. Recently, we had produced a bunch of No Barriers flags, and we told people to bring them out and hold them high at significant moments. I thought this qualified, so I pulled one from the zipper pocket of my dry top and handed it to Arjun. "I want you to have this," I said. "You deserve it."

"Why you crying, Dad?" Arjun asked.

"They're not tears," I said, wiping them away with the back of my hand. "My face is just wet from river water."

"If you say so," he replied.

"I want you to know I'm proud of you, and I think you're very brave," I told Arjun. Then I tousled his hair, gave him a tight hug, and got up quickly before more tears could flow.

23

It seemed almost unreal, like a dream I'd wake up from as soon as I entered the bracingly cold water of the Colorado River. But on September 7, 2014—eight years after first descending the canyon with Harlan Taney, and four years after committing to this adventure while standing atop a mountain with Kyle Maynard—we were finally here at Lees Ferry, our put-in on the Grand Canyon.

I believed I was as ready as I'd ever be, though some doubts still lingered. We all helped unload and organize piles of equipment we'd need for three weeks on the river, from Paco pads and folding chairs to giant ceramic water filters and a three-burner stove. The meat and vegetables had all been frozen solid, and even though the air temperature would most likely top one hundred degrees in the lower canyon, perishables would last the whole trip in superinsulated coolers that were submerged at the bottom of the rafts. At an average of forty-eight degrees, the river water was a natural refrigerator. We also carted out the portable toilets that river people affectionately called "groovers," for the grooves they formed on your butt cheeks. The Grand Canyon was a pristine ecosystem. There were strict regulations about packing out all garbage and human waste. From past trips, I'd gotten used to muddling along narrow, weaving, bouldery trails, through tangles of prickly plants, and past wild visitors like scorpions and rattlers to find the groover, always tucked away in a discreet location at one end of camp.

Once everything had been unloaded, Rob led me through the maze of gear to cool off, and we stood ankle-deep in the icy water, splashing our faces and soaking our caps and bandannas. For a year, I'd been memorizing the river's fabled rapids and their different mileage points, and now their names chanted like a chorus in my head: Hance, Sockdolager, Horn Creek, Granite, Hermit, Crystal, Deubendorff, Upset, and, of course, Lava Falls. Even though it was 179 miles from where I stood, the thought of Lava terrified me. Most people agreed that this four-hundred-yard stretch of raging chaos was the biggest, baddest rapid in the Grand Canyon. In 1869, John Wesley Powell's team had the good sense to portage their gear around it, even though it took three hours of backbreaking work. Then they'd lowered the boats on ropes through the maelstrom. In the modern age, Lava was responsible for more wooden boats splintering, more rubber rafts folding like tacos, and more kayakers swimming for their lives than any other of the rapids.

As I stood there with Rob, I remembered the story Harlan had told us about his first Grand Canyon expedition. Twenty-five years earlier he'd been pitched out of the raft and his mom had clutched his life jacket, desperately clinging to him, right there on the big black Cheese Grater Rock at Lava Falls. The very thought of it made my stomach do flip-flops and made me want to run for the groover. But there were plenty of rapids between Lees Ferry and Lava Falls that could easily hammer me, plenty of whirlpools, boils, holes, and fierce eddy lines. So I told myself not to think too far ahead, just to focus on each day, on every single paddle stroke.

Rob patted me on the back. "Big E, we got this," he said. "The good thing about this canyon is that it warms you up. The rapids get progressively harder each day until Lava when you've been paddling already for two weeks. We're gonna be fine."

Our team of kayakers numbered ten and reflected the history of my progression as a boater. In the midst of his cancer fight, thankfully, Rob was there. Not only would he guide me himself, he would be in charge of creating the plan of attack for each rapid, placing the various team members in the right positions. Rob had been the force behind this entire process, even when I thought the door might be closing, and I owed him everything.

Next, there was Rocky Contos, Steven Mace, and Skyler Williams. Thanks to Sky and my father, Ed, Nature Valley was helping to pay for the expedition and had provided enough granola, nuts, and energy bars to feed an army.

Then there was Timmy O'Neill. And there was Lonnie with his two guides, Seth Dahl and Chris Drew. Even though Lonnie and I each had our own guides, Rob emphasized that ultimately we were all one unified team, with interchangeable parts who would work together to ensure success and safety for all.

My main guide down the river would, of course, be Harlan. How lucky I had been to meet him on that first Grand Canyon trip. His knowledge of "the Big Ditch" was unrivaled. He'd obtained all the permits from the National Park Service and organized raft support. The staff at No Barriers believed it was important to capture the story of the first double-blind descent of the canyon, so Harlan had spent a week customizing a thirty-seven-foot inflatable motorized raft with twelve solar panels that charged an array of batteries with fourteen thousand watts of storage capacity. It was enough to not only power my vital radio communications, but also the four video cameras and four laptop computers to organize and edit the video footage. He'd also created a mobile, lightweight boom as effective as a Hollywood crane—but portable and wireless—that could withstand the rigors of weather and water. To direct the film for No Barriers, I'd invited Michael Brown, who'd made the documentary on our Mount Everest ascent and a film on our first No Barriers expedition in Nepal with a military veteran team. He was well versed in how to capture beautiful stories in rugged environments.

Arizona Raft Adventures—or AzRA for short—organized all our river logistics. Their large, motorized rafts would carry the tons of gear and food so we could concentrate exclusively on safely kayaking the river. AzRA was the same company that had taken me and the blind teenagers down the Grand Canyon with Harlan and Marieke years before, so it was all coming full circle. Since that first trip, the owner, Fred Thevenin, had been a huge supporter and had gone out of his way to make sure we had everything we needed.

When all was ready and the three support boats loaded, we eased into the river under a clear sky. There had been many months of preparation and buildup, so it felt good to finally be on the water. A soft breeze blew against my face. Later in the day, that wind could rage, a result of rising heat that forced the air up the canyon. Often it blew so fiercely, it canceled out the effects of the water current, so you had to fight your way downriver. However, for now, the sun and breeze felt perfect. I did a practice roll, and when I came up, I took a deep breath and listened to the muffled sound of the river funneling skyward, filling the canyon and reverberating off the sheer rock walls to either side. I could already sense the majesty of this place, as well as its menace.

24

As we passed under the Navajo Bridge, just a few miles below the put-in, Rob paddled up to me, excitedly reporting that he had seen a California condor right overhead. Their population had been decimated due to lead poisoning. By 1987, there was just one remaining bird in the wild, but with conservation and reintroduction efforts, they were slowly making a comeback.

"It's a good omen!" Rob said excitedly. "Although I don't really believe in omens," he then corrected himself.

Approaching Badger Creek Rapid, I could hear tourists hooting and hollering from the cliffs five hundred feet above us, wishing us a bon voyage. By now I was concentrating more on the rising murmur of water ahead, and I felt the zing of acceleration under my boat as our team took its positions. Timmy, Steven, and Skyler went through first and then eddied out below the rapid, ready to rescue any swimmers or retrieve any boats or paddles. I went second with Harlan just behind me calling commands in my headset. Rob slipped in behind Harlan, scanning the rapid and keeping an eye on me, ready to swoop in and assume commands should Harlan flip or have any problems of his own. "Easy forward," Harlan called over the radio. "Small left. Now easy right." I bounced over giant wave swells. "Now charge!" Harlan yelled, and a wave hit me unexpectedly from the side. I braced hard and felt myself tipping. Do not flip and swim in your first rapid, I scolded myself. I recovered and managed to stay upright. Sitting in the eddy below Badger, Harlan and Rob eased up to me, and Rob slapped me on the back.

"Nice job, Big E. One rapid down, just 164 to go." Then he let out a big honking laugh that echoed off the canyon walls.

Lonnie's team came through next, with Seth in front and Chris behind, and Lonnie between them. Seth was hollering loud, "On me! On me!" and kept shouting all the way through. Rocky was the last to pull into the eddy. He was serving as sweep, or as we had begun to call it, the "Hail Mary." If all else failed, he'd be the guy to help any stragglers who'd gotten into trouble and had somehow been left behind.

As we paddled out of the eddy and back into the current, the sound of Badger Creek faded slowly behind us, replaced by hoots of encouragement and paddle high fives. Timmy glided up beside Rob and said, "We're under way, Papa Duck. And excellent orchestration of our first rapid, I might add."

"Papa Duck?" Rob repeated.

"Yeah," said Timmy. "You're E's original guide, the man who's most responsible for us all being here. You're the proud daddy who watches over his baby ducklings and makes sure they're safe." Then he patted Rob on the back, leaned in, and said more quietly, "And you are the elder statesman of the team."

We all chuckled, but as I thought about it, the name was perfect. Rob was paternal, not in an overbearing way, but like a good sheepdog watches over his flock, attentive and aware. His role had changed from being my lead guide to now being one of the secondary guides, supporting Harlan. This had actually been Rob's decision. He'd known that Harlan's experience and unparalleled knowledge of the Grand Canyon made him the best choice to guide me. It was a typical Rob Raker maneuver, absolutely devoid of ego, and I respected him even more for it. Though he had stepped back, I knew he would always be nearby, always right behind or on the periphery, watching every move to make sure his team was safe and the trip would go smoothly.

Timmy was right. He was our Papa Duck.

Now on flat water, our flotilla spread out over the wide river. Rob paddled off to see if he could spot more condors or bighorn sheep on the cliffs. The muscles in my arms were already feeling the effect of what would dominate much of the next three weeks: paddling flat water downstream into variable headwinds. Harlan had warned us: "When people envision the Grand Canyon, they only think about white water, but between those rapids, there's a lot of flat water, 91 percent to be exact. So there'll be plenty of time to chat and chill between the carnage."

It was three miles until the next rapid, Soap Creek, so Harlan and I settled into a steady rhythm, rolling underwater every few minutes to stave off the heat. Then I heard a quick splash. Harlan chuckled and said, "E, check this out. Hold out your hands." I lay my paddle across my boat and put my palms up, and he plopped a large, slimy, wriggling trout into my hands. He'd seen it swimming in the clear water and literally plucked it out of the river. I smiled in disbelief before dropping it back. Harlan had such an intimate relationship with this place. I remembered how on our first trip down here, his sister had described him surfing and flipping in the play waves, how he was virtually one with his kayak, and he and his kayak were one with the river. On the Usu, he'd told me that, during one busy year, between guiding biologists and leading private trips, he'd spent over one hundred days down here. He knew every bend, every side canyon, every tributary, every beach, bench, and riffle. I was awed by that kind of deep connection and knowledge.

In the late afternoon, after several more rapids, we reached the Supai Ledges, just as an impressive September squall began pattering raindrops on the flat rock shelves. The patter turned into a full-on deluge, and everyone scurried to set up tents, and some of the boys set up camp in caves between the overhanging ledges of rocks. As sheeting rains cascaded down the canyon walls, it felt like something of a celebration. After a successful first day on the river, most of us stripped down and stood beneath the superheated waterfalls pouring off the cliffs, showering in the warm wash, laughing. The rain came down so hard, I could hear chunks of earth falling from the walls across the river and splashing violently into the water.

I awoke to the morning sun drying the tent and the rock shelves we'd camped on. As we launched our kayaks, the river smelled of earth, and the water felt textured, thick with silt. That silt was already covering my face, in my mouth and eyes, in my underwear and clothing. "The Colorado River has the highest percentage of silt to water of any other river in the world," Harlan said, "and after it rains, it turns to sludge." Rob confirmed that the water had gone from clear, where we'd started near the Glen Canyon Dam, to "chocolate milk."

Shortly, we came to House Rock Rapid, the first considerable rapid of the canyon. It was rated about a 7 on the Grand Canyon 1-to-10 scale. "Stay right, stay right," Harlan warned me as we drew near. But his voice was garbled and choppy over the radios, cutting in and out. Great, I thought, feeling frustration and fear expanding inside me. The first big rapid and the radios are already failing! "Large hole on left! Hard right!" I could barely make out the words through my earpiece.

The force of the water and lack of clear communication put me on the defensive. I tensed up and leaned back, my head cocked awkwardly to the side as I strained to hear. The movement became violent, abrupt, tossing me up and down. Amid the tumult, the paint-shaker motion, and the boomeranging barrage of river noise, I recovered and did what Rob and Harlan had taught me. I paddled hard.

"Charge!" I finally heard Harlan say, muffled and distant. I slammed into a cold wall of water. A powerful lateral wave lurched me sideways as the world tossed and turned in dizzying confusion. "Brace left! Brace left!" Harlan squawked, and I righted myself, half hearing "Charge!" I dug in, air, spray, and sound engulfing me. "You're good, you're good," Harlan's voice crackled as I bounced through the last set of tail waves and eddied out, slumping in relief.

The next ten miles were through the Roaring Twenties, a bunch of big rapids in quick succession. A third of the way through, we stopped at one of the giant waves to try to surf it, one of Harlan's favorite hobbies. We all waited in the eddy, and when it was my turn, Harlan tried to get me angled just right, and then gave a "charge" command to get me paddling hard across the hole, leaning hard and bracing upriver and desperately trying to stay upright. For a moment, I rode the wave laterally, back and forth, before being flipped and flushed out the bottom.

Neither Lonnie nor I had the technique down, but Steven, Rob, and Timmy could stay on the wave for thirty seconds or more, while Harlan managed to stay in the longest, doing spins and cartwheels. I gave up after a few tries, happy to float in the eddy, listening to the yips and critiques of the team, but Lonnie was persistent. He must have charged that hole a dozen times, each time getting flipped, spit out the bottom, and eagerly ready for another try. Lonnie attacked the big rapids like a rodeo cowboy riding a bull.

"Lonnie hit that play wave like the lawn dart that he is," said Timmy. "He's got a sharp point, and he launches in hard and headfirst, ready to impale anything in his way!"

We all laughed, and "LonDart" became his official river name.

25

Throughout the rest of the Roaring Twenties, the radios were driving me crazy and increasing my stress level. Sometimes they worked and sometimes they didn't, and the unpredictability was the most disconcerting aspect.

In Rapid 24.5, a set of powerful waves sent me and my kayak airborne. When I landed in the storm of water, Harlan yelled, and it came out as "Brrrr rttt!" and it took me a second to process that he was saying "Brace right!," but when I leaned right, it was too late. A crashing wave pounded me from the left. I went under, finally rolling back up at the bottom of the rapid. By the end of the Roaring Twenties, the mental tension had translated into physical exhaustion. My upper body was tight, my reactions delayed and imprecise.

When we got to camp, I was quiet and on edge. "A rapid has enough wild cards," I said to Skyler dejectedly. "I don't need another one." In the midst of big, loud chaos, it was so comforting to have a voice in my ear. It gave me confidence. Without that tether to another human being, I felt alone, like that sea of water would engulf me and overpower me. The team gathered on the rocky bank and began troubleshooting, trying to figure out the source of the problem. We could not come up with a clear solution, and the ongoing radio problems continued to jeopardize the trip for me.

Thankfully, the next two days were light on rapids, with long stretches of flat water. Harlan and the other guides could rest their voices, and Steven cleverly attached his iPod to a couple of waterproof speakers, which he slung over his back. Lonnie and I fell in behind him, paddling in rhythm to some high-energy tunes. The music sounded clear and sharp with the beats echoing crisply off the canyon walls. Since following a constant sound was way more efficient than responding and readjusting to voice commands, it made the miles go pretty quickly, except for the occasional times Lonnie and I would unexpectedly collide, paddles clanking or Lonnie's boat spearing mine in LonDart fashion.

At the end of the day, I was pretty fatigued, not only from the burning heat that, in my dry top, made me feel like I was stewing in my own personal sauna, but from concentrating so hard on following Harlan's commands, which were increasingly difficult to decipher through the radios. His voice had begun sounding so distant, it was like he was calling down to me from the moon.

I shouted over to Skyler, "Sky, can you snag me the sat phone?" We'd planned to use it only for emergencies, but I figured failing radios after only a few days of paddling qualified.

We managed to scramble up to an open place on the ledges where we got a decent satellite signal, and I called the radio communications company in the United Kingdom. Luckily, Derek, the owner, answered and readily agreed to express-air two more units. However, a lot of moving parts would need to come together. Derek would have to build and test the units and ship them overnight from Europe. They'd need to clear customs in Phoenix and be driven to Flagstaff. Then Marieke, Harlan's sister, would have to drive them to the South Rim, where one of Harlan's friends would hike them down to Phantom Ranch at the bottom of the canyon. We'd be at Phantom in less than a week, and if there was one mishap in the chain, I'd have no working radios for the biggies that were to follow: Horn Creek, Granite, Crystal, Upset, and, most important, Lava Falls.

That night, the crew hung out pretty late after dinner, telling river stories. As usual, Timmy provided the entertainment by dragging out two giant dry bags, which clanged and jingled. He reached inside and began handing out musical instruments: old guitars, drums, triangles, cowbells, tambourines, and percussive shakers. Everyone took an instrument and began jamming in a circle, with Timmy whimsically leading and improvising lyrics, usually about someone on the trip like Papa Duck or Lonnie the LonDart. Then he'd call out a name and that person would have to make up and sing a verse.

After another day of paddling mostly flat water, we made it into camp with enough time to spend the late afternoon heading up the steep switchback trail to the cliffside Nankoweap Granaries, hundreds of feet above the river. Small hollowed-out rooms were carved into the sheer wall where ancient Pueblo peoples, ancestors of the current-day Hopi, had stored seeds and grain to protect their food source from critters and rot.

As Harlan and I sat on the rocks in front of the ruins, I said, "They must have been an industrious people to carve out a life in this desert."

"They were deeply connected to the river and this canyon," he replied. Then he took my hand and pointed upstream. "They also had salt mines a few miles from here," he said. "Some of the walls are still white as chalk. It was a rite of manhood for Hopi boys to take a pilgrimage from high up on the mesa down to the salt mines. They're sacred grounds."

Just then, the early-evening winds began picking up, descending from the canyon rim. It felt so peaceful up here, I was in no hurry to leave. "This is my home," Harlan continued, "and I want to share it with you."

I had to admit, it was quite an impressive home. I could hear the huge canyon wall across the river and the open expanse of the sky above. Somewhere above I could hear the cry of a red-tailed hawk, and far below, I could hear the ever-present churn of the river as it pressed on toward the sea.

"I'm still afraid," I said, waving my hand in the direction of the river below. "I've tried to fight it, but sometimes I think the fear is winning . . . and the real big rapids are all still ahead."

Harlan paused, and I could tell he was also surveying the river, both upstream and down. "In kayaking, you're interacting with something that is bigger than you," he said, "something that is moving randomly in different directions. No matter how good you get, you can't always predict it. And once you're headed into the rapid, there's no stop button. It's not like other sports where you can throw on the brakes and regroup. Once you've made the decision to go, you have to be okay with it and accept what happens. That's daunting, but I think it's also beautiful. The river does what it does."

"But how do you ever master that mind game?" I asked.

"I think it's a balance between control and letting go," he answered. "Try to control it completely, and the river crushes you. Give in completely, and the river will also crush you. It's ultimately about harnessing its energy and riding it for a moment."

It was time to head back to dinner. As I stood up, brushed off my pants, and began probing my trekking poles for the jumble of descending rocks, I knew tomorrow began the Inner Gorge, and the radios were becoming a lesson in frustration. A wave of nerves passed through my body, but then I focused on my breathing and the soft rush of the river, letting it fill my consciousness. With each exhalation, I felt some of that weight lifting. Maybe, I thought, I'll try it LonDart style.

26

Waking on the seventh day, we had a series of four challenging rapids to navigate in succession, all rated about 8s: Hance, then Sockdolager, Grapevine, and Zoroaster. On the way across the beach to breakfast, I could hear Lonnie on the ground doing his morning ritual of fifty sit-ups, crunches, and push-ups, a military habit he'd stuck with. Feeling nauseous, I nervously choked down some breakfast, as our filmmaker, Michael Brown, asked me, "What are you thinking this morning?"

"I'm actually trying not to think," I answered. After consulting Harlan, Harlan said he felt comfortable guiding me without radios. He'd try to stay right behind me and yell extra loudly. "If we get separated for any reason," he said, "don't panic. Relax. Breathe. Be at peace with the river. You're here, in this moment. Nothing else matters."

A mile out of camp, we came to Hance, a long, left bend in the river with the right side dubbed "the Land of the Giants," a series of big boulders to avoid.

"We'll work from the tongue of smooth water starting out on the right," Harlan said, "then skirt left, avoiding the big, potentially problematic holes created by those rocks."

Somehow I was able to follow Harlan's advice and to execute his directions, angling my boat against the crashing laterals coming off the boulders. I was actually surprised when Harlan yelled, "We're good! We're through it! Now we're just riding the squirrelly water at the bottom!"

Sockdolager was up next, named by Major Powell. It was the phrase used at the time to describe a knockout blow in a boxing match. He was referring to the two massive sequential waves, about twenty feet from trough to crest.

Harlan steered me in and lined me up straight against those waves. "Charge! Charge!" he yelled, and I rode up the first that felt almost vertical, and then down, digging with everything I had, exploding through the next that crashed over my head. I disappeared for a moment in the wall of water and then emerged on the other side into the bright sun. I think I was actually smiling.

After Grapevine and Zoroaster, we arrived at Cremation Camp, about a mile above the famous Phantom Ranch. Long, steep trails from both the North and South Rims of the canyon accessed Phantom, so we were joined now by throngs of hikers, some camping among the cottonwood trees along Bright Angel Creek. Somehow word had gotten out about the two blind kayakers coming down the river, and Lonnie and I posed for photos with several families. From the ranch restaurant, Timmy helped me write a postcard home.

Outside the window of the restaurant, I could hear nearly continuous mule trains carrying supplies up and down the canyon. It
was comforting to know those hoofbeats were the link to my
family. They'd be carrying my postcard almost five thousand feet
up the Bright Angel Trail, and it would arrive back in Colorado in
a few days.

That night, we settled into Cremation Camp, and after dinner,
we began hearing clanking around the kitchen area. There wasn't
enough wind to knock pots and pans over, so Timmy investigated,
shining his light against the rocks. "Ringtail cats!" he exclaimed.
"Two of 'em."

Harlan got up, chucked a rock over in their general direction,
and shooed them away from the kitchen. I could hear them scrambling up onto the sheer rock wall right behind the camp. "Ring-
tails are beautiful, but pesky little critters," he said. He described
them: long, striped tails and big, round ears. "They're nocturnal,
and they get into all kinds of stuff if you leave it out. They'll chew
a hole through a dry bag to get to free food!"

"Reminds me of the coons and possums back home on the
farm," Lonnie added.

Then Harlan asked, "So, Lonnie, how does a farm boy from
Indiana wind up kayaking down the Grand Canyon, anyway?"

Lonnie cleared his throat and said, "Well, it started with meeting the folks from Team River Runner and learning to roll in my
little pond, but really, the truth of it is, it all started with my
daughter Bug and me mowing the lawn."

Everyone smiled, ready for a signature Lonnie joke, but he was
serious this time. He went on, "About three months after I lost my
eyesight, after the accident, I was setting around my house doing

nothin', feelin' sorry for myself, and I got up and decided to go out-side. I had no mobility training, but I found a broomstick and used it to walk out through the yard, toward my barn. But before I got there, I ran into a tussle of weeds, about up to my chest. So I turned around and went back up to the house. My youngest daughter was standing there. Her name's Taylor, but I call her Bug. She was five years old at the time.

"She looked up at me, and she said, 'Daddy, what's wrong?' I said, 'Nothing, Bug.' Now, I couldn't see her, but I'm convinced she put her one hand on her hip and pointed her little finger at me. She said, 'Yeah, there is, Daddy. Tell me what's wrong!' I was getting called out by a five-year-old. I said, 'Well, Bug, if you got to know, I'm just a little frustrated. I can't get into my barn without walk-ing through all those dern weeds, and I can't see to mow them.' She looked at me, and she said, 'Daddy, I'll help you.' I said, 'All right, girl, if you got the guts, take my finger, lead me to the ga-rage.'"

I imagined this feisty little mini-Lonnie leading him through the grass.

"Bug led me around to the garage," Lonnie told us. "I had my truck parked outside, but she led me around it and lifted up the big door into the garage where I stored my riding lawn mower. I said, 'Take me to the mower.' She took me over there. I got on it, put her on my lap, fired it up, out the door we went. Then she yelled, 'Stop!' I said, 'What?' She said, 'The truck.' I said, 'Where is it?' She said, 'Right there.' I said, 'Right where?'"

Lonnie had me now. I was leaning forward on my folding chair in anticipation. "I said, 'Point at it.' She pointed at it, and I felt her little arm. I turned the wheel, backed up, turned it the other way, and took off. Then I heard, 'Stop, the tree! Stop, the fuel tank!' 'Okay, Bug. If we got to go left or right, you start turning the wheel that direction. I'll feel it, and I'll help you.' She drove me right out to the barn. I had her get off the lawn mower, go back up to the house, and watch."

I was cringing, just waiting for him to collide into the side of the barn, or worse.

"I got my hand on the side of the barn, squared it up, and mowed a lap. Then I took that broomstick, held it against the barn and mowed a second lap. I held it all the way out and mowed the third lap. I shut the lawn mower off, and I went back up to the house. I could hear Bug just squealing, 'You did it, Daddy, you did it! I knew you could do it!' I picked her up and give her a big hug.

"About two minutes later, my dad pulled up into the driveway. He said, 'Who mowed around the barn?' I said, 'Tell him, Bug.' She told him, and he got mad, I mean furious. He said, 'I told you, if you ever need anything done around here, you let me know and I'll do it.' I said, 'No, Dad. You realize what just happened here?'

"He said, 'You mowed around your barn?' I said, 'No. Much more than that.'"

Lonnie's voice got softer, almost a whisper, and there was a deep pride in it. "I said, 'Do you see that little girl standing right there? To that little girl right there, and to her two sisters, my name is still Daddy. To that little girl right there and her two sisters, I'm still the man. To that little girl and her two sisters, I still can.'"

Everyone was quiet, soaking it all in. Then Lonnie asked, "Now, when I look into the mirror, you know what I see?"

Steven answered, "You see pride for everything you've overcome?"

"No," Lonnie replied. "I'm blind. I don't see nothin' in there."

Everyone laughed and groaned. He chuckled and then went on, "When we get up every day and we look in the mirror, we have to see worth. We have to see value. We have to see we're needed, we're loved, and we can make a difference.

"And when I look in the mirror now, I say, 'Yeedog, you're getting better-looking all the time!'"

Lonnie guffawed and then said, "That day I got shot in the face, well, I thought the world had come to an end, but thanks to a child, I took a step, and the world was still there."

27

Since Rob's cancer diagnosis, he'd been learning how dairy and animal fats could accelerate the spread of prostate cancer, and he'd been trying to eliminate them. But he also knew that, unlike sparse mountain provisions, a river trip was full of temptation: chicken alfredo, steak fajitas with sour cream and shredded cheese, bread doused with garlic butter, and carrot cake and berry crumble. So Rob had made it his No Barriers Pledge to restrict his diet to fruit, veggies, and fish during the entire trip. However, various team members had already been catching him break his vow, sneaking chunks of salami and cheddar. At breakfast, I was right behind him. He had just loaded a pile of bacon onto his plate when Steven Mace—burly, bearded, and barrel-chested—cut in front of me, leaned into Rob, and said, "Hey, Rob, I have something for you."

Rob's eyes must have been preoccupied by the display of food on the table, because he asked, "What's that?"

"It's a river rock, and I want you to keep it in your pocket at all times," Steven said. "It'll be a reminder of your pledge. When you're feeling weak and about to break, grab it and hold it. Squeeze it tight, and it will help summon up your inner strength, your inner resolve."

"Cool," I said, "like the challenge coins they give out in the military."

"Yeah," Steven said, "your Grand Canyon challenge rock."

"Thanks, Steven. That's thoughtful," Rob said, sliding it into his pocket. "I'll start it at lunch." Then he reached for the bacon on his plate, but before Rob's hand landed on a piece, Steven snatched the entire pile off the plate and stuffed it into his mouth. Then he squeezed Rob's shoulder firmly and, between the smacking and chewing, managed to say, "Rob, you stay strong now."

I didn't laugh long, because Harlan sat down next to me and said, "It's a big day ahead, E. We've got Horn Creek, Granite, and Hermit, all rated 9s and all within a five-mile stretch." As I listened, I was barely managing to choke down my breakfast, leaving the bacon on my plate half-eaten. "We're just gonna take them one at a time. Horn Creek is up first, just a couple of miles downriver. It's got the steepest drop in the Grand Canyon. At this water level, these two big rocks jut out side by side. Some people say they look like horns, but, with the water pouring over them, I think they look more like big glassy domes or camels' humps; they are some of the most beautiful water features in the river. We'll shoot the gauntlet between them and take a few sizable hits. We want to avoid what's below, if possible: a maze of big waves, rocks, and holes. So we're going to be making a hard cut to the left; I'll call it out, guiding us away from those powerful, tricky hydraulics. But if we can't make the left move, we'll pivot and then just take those big crashers head-on."

"Sounds like a plan," I said, unable to take another bite. My eggs rumbled in my belly and were about to turn into a vomit omelet.

Once on the water, we passed under the Kaibab Bridge leading to Phantom Ranch, and pulled over. There was news to celebrate. The new—and hopefully improved—radios had arrived. Harlan's mom had found a courier to drive them from Phoenix halfway to Flagstaff, where Marieke had met the driver on the side of the road. Marieke had then relayed them to a good friend of Harlan's who drove to the South Rim and hiked them down the steep, nine-mile Bright Angel Trail, where he hand delivered them to us, just in time. Skyler opened the box to check that everything was there. I just hoped they worked. I was going to need them.

Sooner than expected, I heard the distant rush of Horn Creek ahead. "We're gonna angle in from right center," Harlan said, "and split the horns."

I could hear him fairly clearly in my earpiece, which helped me try to stay calm. I floated tentatively down a perfectly smooth tongue, like riding a moving sidewalk that you knew was leading you into a category-five hurricane. Then the bow of my boat dipped, and I dropped off the edge of the earth, accelerating into the storm. I paddled harder, leaning forward and squaring off against the big hits.

As I continued to find myself upright, I felt some confidence rising. When Harlan gave the word, I edged left, leaning downriver and bracing my paddle against the surging waves. Then water exploded on top of me, and it hurled me over. Upside down, I waited for it to release me, and when I felt its energy subsiding, I rolled up, bracing for more action. Instead, I was surprised to hear the cheers of the team and Harlan. I was through it, through Horn, a rapid with a fearsome reputation.

There wasn't much time to celebrate, because the next thing I knew, we were entering the thunder of Granite. It had a strong pull to the wall on river right, with waves coming fast from both directions. I managed to remain upright, staying loose and reacting to the punches striking me from either side. Yet as I bucked and bounced, Harlan's voice went silent for several seconds. No radios! my brain screamed, but then I heard something faint, almost like static: "Blr-glrgshshsh." *Harlan*, I realized, was upside down! I sensed I was pointing in the right direction, so I just kept charging. Then there was a louder sound, a gasping breath, and Harlan's voice resumed: "Small left . . . charge!"

As I paddled into the tail waves that led me out of Granite, I thought, Even Harlan can get rocked by this river.

Up next was Hermit, which Harlan noted had the biggest waves in the canyon. "Think of it as a big, fun wave train," he said. But that "fun" included about a dozen waves in succession, some of them over twenty feet tall. As I dipped down into the troughs, I tried to keep my kayak pointed straight. Then I felt myself rushing up a wall of water so steep I was certain I would flip over backward. "Hang on!" Harlan yelled. "Lean forward!"

I pressed my torso against the hull of my kayak and managed not to tip. My kayak caught air off the lip of that three-story wave, and I straightened up for the big drop into the next one.

At the bottom eddy, Lonnie and I compared notes. We'd both flipped once, but then Skyler mentioned he'd gone over three times. "Blind guys rule! Sighted people drool!" I shouted to Lonnie, reaching out and finding his hand for a fist bump. We both pumped our fists in the air and cheered to Skyler's amused chagrin.

After a stop at camp, we headed out again and immediately encountered a six-mile stretch called the Gems: six rapids, spaced one per mile—Agate, Sapphire, Turquoise, Emerald, Ruby, Serpentine. Although they were giant, they retained a feeling of friendliness. There were no monster holes or complex navigation to twist my gut. I just had to point 'er straight and ride the bucking river serpent.

After the excitement, Harlan had us pull over to a spot he'd discovered on one of his previous trips. He told us that the heavy thunderstorms early in the expedition might just awaken something special. We hiked along the beach, through some tamarisk bushes, and came to an alcove with a giant bedrock pothole that had been filled in with rainwater.

"Shhhhh," Harlan instructed. "Sit down and await the surprise." Within seconds, on cue, a cacophony of croaks emanated from the pond, as if Harlan the conductor had just waved his baton. We laughed hard, and then someone stupidly chucked a rock in the pond, probably thinking the frogs would respond by croaking again. Instead, they went totally silent, and I feared that had ended our encounter. Then Timmy let out his own frog song: "*Err err err err, err err err err. BREEDEET.*" He simultaneously screeched and rolled out a clear click in the back of his throat. It was a near-perfect impression, and the frogs all belched right back at him, like they had a new leader.

Lonnie whispered, "Timmy, I'd be careful. I think they're in love with you."

"That's right," Harlan said. "That's their mating call, and looks like Timmy's got a few hundred admirers over there."

"I'm going to live here forever and be the Frog King," said Timmy. As he continued to croak, and his groupies continued to call back in rapture, I began losing track of who was who. For a blind person, this was a symphonic masterpiece of nature, and we all sat back enjoying the show for over an hour.

28

Just before camp that evening, we reached a beautiful side canyon called Elves Chasm that Harlan wanted us to experience. We hiked up a damp, lush creek bed with several small waterfalls created by boulders that choked the channel. Several shelves up, we came to a deep pool with a tall waterfall pouring down. We all took turns swimming over and letting the clear fresh water pour over our heads, washing the sand out of our hair and faces. Behind the waterfall was an actual chasm, cool and damp from the water spray. We scrambled inside, and tucked ten feet back was a climb through a small, body-wide window that popped you into the sun again. From there, we carefully walked out on ledges to stand fifteen feet above the pool. As Lonnie and I hovered, toes curled over the lip, Timmy shouted directions, playing on our kayak commands: "Small left, gun sites on me. Now charge!" And then we'd leap into the air, plunging toward the pool.

Afterward, Lonnie and I sat in the back of the cave behind the waterfall. I tapped the rock ceiling right above my head and said, "It's kind of claustrophobic in here. Anything like the inside of a submarine?"

"Sure is," he agreed. "I was stationed on those attack subs for five years of my military career. Talk about confined spaces—on one of those deployments, the sub was diving, and I was cleaning the frame bay; that's like the ribs of the sub, underneath the main sump. Well, our tactical situation required us to dive quickly. Problem is that submarines compress with the water pressure. In other words, as the sub descends, the chamber gets smaller, and I mean mighty small. I was in a bad place, between one of those metal ribs and the sump, about to turn into Flatbread Lonnie. So I quickly rolled into the frame bay between the ribs, a spot with just enough room where I wasn't going to get squashed. I was stuck there, lying on my back."

"How long?" I dared to ask.

"Quite some time," he said, laughing at the recollection. "I suspect, fifteen or sixteen hours."

I shuddered, thinking that being flipped upside down in a kayak was nothing compared to being practically compressed to death in a submarine. "Some of the guys brought me some blankets," he said, "and reached in to hand me a pee bottle and some food. I told them that pancakes would fit the occasion." He guffawed again. "I just had to wait long enough for us to surface again and for the hull space to expand."

"How'd you get through it?" I asked. "Did you meditate or something?"

"Every now and then, one of the crew would holler down at me to see that I was okay, but other than that, I didn't meditate; I didn't count sheep. I just lay there sort of daydreaming. It was great training on how to stay calm in tight spaces and not panic—like, upside down and out of air in a big ole keeper hole!" He cackled.

The story was vintage Lonnie. While most people would have been so rattled they would have found their sanity slipping away, Lonnie was eating pancakes and cracking jokes with the crew. I didn't think that mind-set was anything he had learned. I suspected, when it came right down to it, he was just hardwired that way. He was a blind man who worked as a roofer, drove a mower, and ran a chain saw. Earlier on the trip, he'd told me more details about the day he got shot in the face. While his friend ran for help, Lonnie lay on the ground totally blind. He could feel blood running down his throat and beginning to clot there and knew that he might very well pass out due to the blood loss. If he did, that blood would coagulate in his throat and choke him. So he'd clawed around, eventually finding a tree limb lying in the dirt. He snapped a branch off and shoved it down his throat, the only way to clear his airway. Turns out, he lay there for hours and did wind up passing out. His clear presence of mind had saved his life. Whether being squeezed in the hull of a submarine or being blinded by shotgun pellets, Lonnie just took action and did what needed to be done, and that ability had made him ideally suited for kayaking. In fact, Lonnie's new trick was to go ahead of his guides through some of the more moderate rapids, without commands. He called it "blind freestyle."

I had to admit, I was a little jealous. Like it or not, I just didn't have "the LonDart" boldness inside me. However, I still wanted to understand the nature of fear, how to stop it from paralyzing me, turning my belly sour, and weighing me down, like struggling through an atmosphere with massive gravity.

I often thought about all I had to lose by making a dumb or reckless mistake. I loved my family, my life; I loved growing the No Barriers movement; I loved waking up, stepping outside my front door, and feeling the cool fresh Colorado morning air combined with that touch of warm sun as it climbed higher in the sky. The thought of leaving it all behind continually consumed me. I had promised my family that I would always be there for them. I couldn't break that promise.

29

That afternoon, we laid over at Dune Camp, around mile 120, a tiny spit of sand so sun scorched you had to wear booties so you didn't burn your feet. The arrival of the new radios had brought such promise, but now, to my intense frustration, they were also beginning to degrade. Harlan's voice was scratchy and distant—just like it had been with the previous sets. Skyler and Steven tinkered with them, trying out different headsets with different manpacks, but they were stumped.

The wind was picking up as Timmy dragged out the musical instruments, and as he started thumping on the bongos, it hit for real: hot, powerful gusts that kicked up sand.

"Boys, I don't think there's going to be any music tonight," Harlan said, "unless someone brought wind chimes. It's time to lash stuff down, put your dry bags in your tents, and dive in. It's about to blow."

We all scrambled to grab gear that was laid out to dry on boats, hanging over tamarisk branches and strewn over rocks. Within minutes, everyone was in their tents, zipping up doors and windows and settling in for a hot wind scouring. Without ventilation, the tent was an oven. The wind howled so hard down the canyon that the tent kept lifting up and tugging at the stakes holding it down. I had endured plenty of hours in the mountains, waiting out bad weather, yet never had the storm been inside my tent! Somehow, the sand had found its way inside and was swirling around in mini-cyclones. I felt grit peppering me all night long, getting into my eyes, ears, and nostrils. I finally put a T-shirt over my face, but it didn't seem to help much. I could feel sand in my teeth and in my throat. I lay there most of the night, sweating on top of my sleeping bag and listening to the tent rattling and the wind roaring and whining outside.

When I awoke the next morning and crawled outside, Timmy and Harlan started chuckling. "You might want to douse yourself off in the river," Harlan said. "You're looking a little crusty."

"More like the Abominable Sandman," Timmy added.

I ran my hand over my face and arms. I was caked with sand from head to toe, and my hair felt stiff like straw.

"Hey!" said Harlan, now animated. "I have an idea I want to test." Apparently he was still looking at me, because he chuckled one more time before he walked over, grabbed the radios that were lying on a tarp, and brought them over to the giant ceramic water filter. He filtered a couple of gallons of river water and filled a big bucket. "This water is super clear now," he pronounced as he submerged one of the radio sets and let it soak for several seconds.

Rob peered into the bucket and remarked, "That's amazing," and he described the clean filtered water turning to the color of café au lait. "The comm systems are waterproof," Rob said, "but looks like silt and sand have been completely clogging the membranes and getting into the microphones, too."

Rob high-fived Harlan and said, "Nice job, Harlan. You should be an engineer."

After thoroughly soaking and drying all the other systems, the sound quality on the radios seemed to bounce back. They weren't as good as new, but they were good enough to get me through. For extra protection, Skyler took little latex covers for injured fingers from the medical kit, covered the foam microphones, and sealed around the edges with tiny, tightly coiled rubber bands.

At breakfast, I chuckled when I heard Steven yelling, "Raker, where's your rock?" I knew Rob must have been caught reaching for some sausage.

"I think it's in my tent," Rob stammered.

Steven sprinted ten feet across the sand and found a rock pile. He swiped one up and replied, "Well, here's another one. Don't lose it. Oh, and I'll take that sausage patty there," and he snatched it off Rob's plate.

The next few days were spectacular as we dropped down into the deepest and oldest part of the canyon. As I ran my hands over the ancient schist, almost two billion years old, jutting straight up from the river, Harlan said, "Welcome to the basement of the Grand Canyon." Some of the schist was smooth as marble through weathering and erosion; other sections were fluted and corrugated, and still others were scalloped and rippled from many millennia of being scoured by waves. We also entered Granite Narrows, the tightest section of the canyon at just seventy-five feet across. The walls here rose a mile above us.

Still in the narrows, we passed a feature called Helicopter Eddy. It was a super-turbulent, violently recirculating eddy formed by a cutout in the rock wall river left. Harlan said emphatically that we wanted to avoid it. It had a toilet bowl effect and could shove you up against the canyon wall and pin you there, and if you were able to dislodge yourself from the wall, the eddy fence was huge and roiling, making it extremely difficult to get back into the river.

However, just above it, Lonnie's guide Chris got slammed in the face by a wave that dislodged his contact lenses and rendered him temporarily blind. In that split second, Lonnie unintentionally paddled over the eddy fence and found himself spinning and smacking into the wall. I could hear his guides yelling from below, unable to help. It was impossible to paddle upriver. But Lonnie yelled back "I'm good!" as he bounced off the wall and braced hard, surfing the eddy fence for a moment. Then, luckily, the eddy spit him out the bottom, and he shot out upright, hooting and laughing.

"That was more fun than a tornado in a trailer park!" he said. "The most fun I've had since I went blind."

I just shook my head.

Just before reaching camp, we pulled into a little side creek that drained out of Matkatamiba Canyon, one of the highlights of the entire journey. We pulled our kayaks up onto a small gravel beach and took a hike that entered a narrowing and twisting slot canyon. Soon the limestone walls were so close I could spread my arms and easily touch both sides. Lonnie and I scrambled together up the smooth, tight groove, which shrunk even more. In places, the bottom was barely a shoe's width wide, and we had to climb above the tiny stream. To make it easier, I showed Lonnie a climbing technique called "stemming," in which you spread both legs wide and press your feet against the rocks. The oppositional force keeps you from sliding down. Lonnie caught on to stemming quickly, and we moved upward, splaying our hands and feet.

Soon, we arrived at a massive amphitheater that flattened out into a natural rock patio. The entire place was a blind man's dream, with curves, grooves, and striations to touch and acoustics that seemed perfectly suited to Tarzan yells. The walls were also excellent for bouldering, with distinct extruding holds, deep indentations, and tiny shelves. Rob and I showed Lonnie some bouldering techniques, and I climbed twenty feet up the sidewall, coaxing Lonnie upward behind me. As we ascended, I loudly slapped the good handholds and coached him how to place his toes in the pockets and to stand up, trusting his feet and balance. Getting back down was even more challenging, and I climbed below him, guiding his feet into the right positions. Lonnie said that, with his girls out of the house, he wanted to try all kinds of adventure sports, from ice climbing to tandem mountain biking, but especially rock climbing. I promised him that when we were back home, I'd have him out to Colorado to cut his teeth in the big mountains.

Back on the ground, I said, "I hope this is just the start of many adventures together," and I squeezed his calloused hand.

"Thank you, brother," he replied. "I can't tell you what an honor it is to be here with you. It means the world to me!"

30

That night at Matkat Hotel Camp, most of the team had gone to bed early, but Lonnie, Timmy, Harlan, and I stayed up late trading stories.

"Upset's got me pretty nervous," I said. "I think we hit it tomorrow." Upset was one of the top-five rapids with many adversity stories to its name. I'd been fretting over it for the last few days.

"On one of my trips down here," Timmy said, "I went through Upset and got the bright idea of trying to punch the big center hole. I was instantly flipped and subbed."

"Subbed" was kayaker talk for being sucked way down and usually held there.

"I felt my boat being pulled down," Timmy went on, "and I was getting pummeled. It seemed like an eternity, but it was probably just ten seconds or so. Then I bobbed to the surface, but before I could roll up, I sensed my boat going down deep again for another beating. I thought seriously about pulling my skirt and swimming, but just when I thought I couldn't hold on a second longer, it released me. I emerged on the other side and rolled up. I was probably under there for twenty-five seconds."

"I know that hole intimately," Lonnie said excitedly. "On my first trip here with Team River Runner, my guide said, 'Lonnie, whatever you do, don't get squirrely and drop into the big hole in the center.' So what do I do? Get squirrelly and drop right into the big hole center. Took my first swim right there in Upset. Boys, I was plenty upset in Upset!"

We all laughed at his joke, corny or not. "But tomorrow's a new day!" he exclaimed. "And you know what I like to say: 'Don't bleed before you're cut.'"

I thought about how to achieve that state. For some people, I thought, it just came naturally. For others, it wasn't so easy. Then Timmy got up to help Lonnie find his tent, and it was just Harlan and me.

"In those first years I guided down here," Harlan said quietly, "after everybody would go to sleep, I would sit on the back of my boat and watch the river cruising by in the moonlight. I know this must sound crazy, but I'd watch the current, and I'd feel an almost uncontrollable impulse to dive in, to disappear, and to see where it took me. After that experience, it was like I'd formed a relationship with the river. Every trip I've paddled since, the last thing I do is to put my hand in the water, and I get that same yearning, the feeling of the current moving through my fingers, moving downstream. It's like a little conversation. I say, 'I'll come back someday, but for now, I've got some more life to live.' This is the place where I'll return someday, and that feels okay, like the river will take care of me."

As I retreated to my tent, I was conflicted. I kept mulling over what Harlan had said, and I couldn't figure out whether the river was an ominous demon or whether it was an entity I could trust, one that was inviting me forward. When did you fight the river with everything you had, and when could you trust it and ride the flow? I still didn't know.

I tried to relax with some music on my iPhone. On my playlist, I was happy to find Mandy Harvey, a professional singer who also happened to be deaf and who I had met when she performed at a No Barriers Summit. Now I was listening to her latest song, which had the same lilting, soothing feel as her previous work. As a result of her experience at the No Barriers Summit, Mandy had taken another courageous step and had begun writing original songs. The outcome was "Try":

> I don't feel the way I used to
> The sky is gray much more than it is blue
> But I know one day I'll get through
> And I'll take my place again
> If I would try
> If I would try
> I don't love the way I need to
> You need more and I know
> That much is true
> So I'll fight for our breakthrough
> And I'll breathe in you again
> So I will try
> So I will try
> There is no one for me to blame

'Cause I know the only thing in my way
Is me . . . so I will try, so I will try . . .

As I listened to her high, angelic voice, I was astounded. It was impressive enough to sing standards and jazz classics you'd heard in a past life with working ears, but it was another world entirely to compose and perform music as a deaf musician. The irony was that they were songs she would never actually hear. It seemed preposterous, like a boat that purposely gives up its mooring, floating on an ocean with no rudder or anchor or any tools to navigate, yet it still expects to sail toward its destination. That bold act moved beyond logic, into the realm of faith, like giving in to the unknowable, like kayaking a river you would never see. No matter how hard you tried, you could never truly see the canyon unfolding before you or the impact you made within it. The journey was incomprehensible.

31

When we reached Upset the next day, Harlan had everyone land and hop out to scout. Upset was already significant, but at this water level, thirteen thousand cfs, he said it got even trickier and more dangerous. He pulled me aside and spoke in a clear, measured voice. "Okay, it's pretty spicy, but there's a perfect line to snake it cleanly, although it'll feel counterintuitive. The setup is everything. You enter left, and you keep pushing left into these lateral waves. They're actually crashing off the left cliff wall. Your brain is telling you don't go over there, but you have to go left. That big hole Lonnie and Timmy were talking about is to your right, and it is violent; it's a place you don't want to be. You want to hit the lateral perfectly on the left, catch the current, and sneak by the big hole on your right. Bam. Done. You got this, E!"

I nodded, but in reality I just kept thinking about that "violent" hole that had subbed Timmy and where Lonnie had swum, the place where you didn't want to be.

We got back into our boats. The safety guides paddled into position, and mercifully, as Harlan said "Check, check," the radios were working. "E, don't let your mind get in the way here," I heard Harlan's soothing voice say. "Your mind can be the barrier between you and the river, between thinking it and just feeling it and being there with it. If your mind gets in the way, then you're defeating the purpose of what this experience is about."

I let his words wash over me, nodding, slowing my breathing, pushing the fear to the outside edges of my awareness.

"I want you to try something," he went on. "Forget that I'm here, that I'm giving you commands to follow. Think of my voice as a line of communication to the water, as a conduit to the river. Allow yourself to feel the intricacies of the rapid. Envision the tongue, like a runway, as we drop in. Imagine the waves, the canyon light glimmering off them, foam and spray igniting in flashes of color and light. Feel the power of the big, green, beautiful waves. Try to truly be here, not fighting against it, not surviving it, but connected to this place. I'll be right behind you to share everything that we're doing."

"Okay," I said, listening hard to the deep rumble below and trying to feel the surface of the water through the bottom of my boat. I sat up, exhaled, and tried to pull some of the river's energy into my lungs. Then we were paddling toward Upset.

"Be clear, calm, in the moment," Harlan said.

I focused on each paddle stroke, each riffle of the water, and the space between each breath. Time seemed to slow down just a bit as I dropped in, turning left and left and left against the massive waves surging off the canyon wall and collapsing over me. I busted through the cold wall of water and heard Harlan yell, "Hold that line!" I felt myself riding on a narrow seam, just between a swirling upheaval to my left, like bombs exploding on a battlefield, and the bottomless hole churning to my right, like a roar coming up from the depths of the river.

I rode the chaos, water, spray, and air all merging together, and it didn't feel as threatening, because I felt like I was a part of it. There was no kayaker, no boat, no paddle, just pure awareness, reacting without conscious thought. Then everything grew calm around me, and I knew the river had allowed me to pass through. I felt gratitude and joy flooding through my body, like current through the canyon.

Then Rob and Harlan paddled over and flanked me, both leaning in, the three of us hugging tightly. No one said a word for a long time. Then Harlan laughed, but not like hearing the punch line of a joke. Instead, it seemed to come from a long way away and carry with it the resonance of deep emotion. "E, I have to admit, most of the time, you and me look like a junk show out there. We're slingshotting by each other; one of us is often backward or sideways, but today, we were in perfect sync. Today, we found the flow!"

That evening at Tuckup Camp, the blazing sun finally passed behind the canyon rim, and the air grew soft and still. I sat on the sand, alone, at the river's edge, reflecting on my experience at Upset. It felt like six years of kayaking culminating in one brief but perfect moment, and I wanted to remember, to bask in it for a little longer. Harlan had said the river was too big to fight against. My ongoing dreams had been of the river swallowing me, pulling me down into darkness, into nothingness.

Climbing mountains hadn't really prepared me either, I thought. Climbing was more about bringing yourself forth, asserting your will over an extreme, inhospitable environment. Yet trying to apply that learning to rivers had failed. Perhaps, the secrets of a river were not revealed by trying to exert the ego over it, but rather by letting go and allowing the river to consume you, all the way down to the core, by simply giving in to the unknowable and writing music you would never hear. By surrendering, it allowed the river to erode everything and wash away the crust, until there was nothing left but that inner light, the same one I had felt many years ago within Terry Fox. Unencumbered, that light was free to flow out and fuse with the landscape, with the energy of the unstoppable river. Maybe this was as close as we could ever get to understanding, just a brief mortal flash of that light connecting with something bigger, something mysterious and infinite.

32

That evening, I asked Rob what made Lava Falls so challenging. In a river renowned for its powerful rapids, Lava definitely got the most attention and respect. It was the king of the canyon.

"Rapids form in three distinct ways," he replied. "First, there's a narrowing of the river channel. Next, there's an elevation drop, in this case about thirty feet from top to bottom. Both of these increase the velocity and turbulence of the current. And third, there's an uneven riverbed where boulders, shelves, drop-offs, and solidified bodies of magma all obstruct the water underneath the surface. Lava Falls is an example of all three factors coming together in a perfect storm. It's rated 10 out of 10 at all water levels."

"In March of 1995," Harlan added, "there was a massive debris flow, like a flash flood on steroids. A monumental rainstorm sent soil and rock, all the way up to boulders the size of SUVs, cascading down Prospect Canyon, left of Lava. That event constricted the river by about 50 percent."

"What was it like before that debris flow?" I asked.

"It was always big," Harlan said, "and it's different from the rapids upriver, because of the volcanism. Over the last 750,000 years, give or take, about a dozen huge lava flows poured down into the Colorado River. Others upwelled from beneath the surface. The magma cooled and formed these sediment-filled lava dams. Near where Lava Falls is today, there was a massive one, a thousand feet tall. They say it plugged the river and backed it all the way up to Lees Ferry—mile one. The lava dam was so enormous, they think it may have taken over twenty years to fill in the lake behind it.

"But even that colossal wall of hardened lava was eventually carved away by the river," said Harlan. "It kept pushing and pushing until it eroded the lava and broke its way through. Nothing stops the river in the end."

Then Rob interrupted, "Enough talk about Lava. Big E, we have some celebrating to do."

I had turned forty-six years old that day, and the team had planned a night of revelry. At dinner, Rob was quietly heading back to his folding chair with a steak on his plate when Steven yelled over, "Raker, where's your rock?"

Rob mumbled something about having lost it again.

"That's the third 'challenge rock' you've lost," said Steven. "If I didn't know you better, I'd think you were losing them on purpose!" With that, he jumped up, blocking Rob's way. I imagined Rob's eyes darting left and right, desperately grasping at escape routes. Then Steven said more gently, "I guess we can make an exception, just this one night, in honor of E's birthday, but tomorrow, don't forget your rock at breakfast."

I didn't have to see to know that Steven's statement had planted a relieved smile on Rob's face.

For dessert, one of the guides had baked a chocolate cake in the Dutch oven, and everyone sang "Happy Birthday" as I blew out the candles. The team had thought of everything. Then Rob led Lonnie and me over to a flat area on the beach where he'd created what he called a "tactile art gallery," comprised of natural objects he'd been collecting along the river.

"Cool," Timmy chimed in. "It's the Grand Canyon Natural Art Museum for the Blind. We gotta take this on the road."

Rob excitedly pronounced that the challenge was for Lonnie and me to examine each exhibit and try to identify it. "I've assembled a unique collection of pieces for your Brailling pleasure."

I chuckled. Rob was referring to an ongoing team joke, of course, started by Timmy. When the guides set up the lunch table on the beach with all the fixings for sandwiches, Lonnie and I would line up with the team, our hands probing over the table. From a sighted perspective, I could understand how our fingers might have looked like little wriggling snakes as they explored the bread, cheese, ham, pickles, and onions. Once, my hand landed on the rim of an unknown jar, opened on the table. I did the natural thing, which was to lick my finger, discovering that it was mayonnaise, but after that, Timmy had begun calling it "Braille lunch."

"Since there's no mayonnaise in this museum," Timmy said, "you can Braille to your heart's content."

I dropped to my knees to explore the first object. It was placed artfully on a large, flat pedestal of rock. The item was made of wood, thin and curvy, and widening toward one end into a round dish. I traced my finger around the circular hollow where the dish part had been perfectly carved by the elements.

"Maybe some kind of horn, like a saxophone?" I said. Then Lonnie, who was kneeling right behind me, agreed with my guess.

Each piece was so beautiful; if I hadn't had an audience, I could have touched them forever. It was hard to believe these chunks of wood had been shaped through years of being tumbled about and scoured by water, sand, and wind until they became hard, almost like they'd been petrified, and as burnished as porcelain. One of them was channeled by dozens of tiny worms boring their way through. Another felt like a head complete with eyes, nose, and a squiggly mouth. Protruding from the top were knots of tangled roots, like dreadlocks. Resting on a flat rock sat a judge's gavel, or maybe, I thought, a glossy peace pipe. Everyone passed it around, pretending to take puffs.

At the end of the line, I was bursting with appreciation. I'd never received a birthday gift quite like this one. I imagined Rob, over the last week, stealthily pulling off the river on various deserted beaches, combing the nooks and crannies, his bushy eyebrows lifting and his face lighting up as he discovered new specimens. Then he carefully placed them in his cockpit until it must have resembled a jungle of crisscrossing designs. Later, slipping away from camp, he exhaustively sorted and paired the objects into the most unique treasures and then displayed them in the most fluid and logical order—all for the Brailling pleasure of two blind friends.

I pulled my attention from the peace pipe in my hands and said, "I can't believe you've been assembling this. I had no idea."

"You're blind," he said matter-of-factly. "It wasn't actually that hard to get away with!" And then he let out his biggest honk of a laugh and slapped me on the back.

When the others had drifted away, Rob and I sat in the sand with our feet in the chilly water and our backs against a steep hillock of sand. "I've been meaning to tell you something, Big E," Rob said. My heart jumped, remembering when he'd first told me about his cancer diagnosis. I braced myself for more bad news.

"I don't talk about this much," he said, "but the last few years have been hard ones. I pride myself on being a problem solver, being able to always find a solution. But I'm faced now with an overwhelming situation. There's no clear way forward.

"But I look at you, the way you deal with your own setbacks, whether it's the death of your mom and your brother, or going blind, or the challenges in your family. Instead of getting beaten down or mired in depression, you've done the absolute opposite. It's like there's a storm in front of you, and you turn into it, instead of away from it."

"A big part of why I'm able to do these things," I said, "is because of you and the team." I waved my hand toward the camp.

"I know how appreciative you are," he replied, "and you know I've enjoyed helping you learn to kayak. I kind of thrive on it. But I've gotten just as much in return. I try every day to adopt that approach: not to let the darkness seep in. I say to myself, 'Okay, this is the situation. This is your choice.' I can either be pissed off and bitter and let circumstances drag me down, or I can say, 'Okay, I have less time than I may have thought. Let's see how much fun, how much excitement, how much joy we can pack in right to the end!'"

"We've definitely packed a lot in," I said, smiling, reflecting on all our shared experiences.

"I've been your guide on a lot of adventures," he resumed, "but you're guiding me as well." He paused, clasped my hand, and cleared his throat. "Thank you, Big E."

I didn't know what to say, but fortunately, I didn't have to, because Rob continued, "And there are some others who want to thank you as well." As if on cue, Skyler came over, sat down, and laid three letters in my hands. "They're from your fam," he said. "They've been stashed away in my dry box."

I missed my family deeply and wished they were here with me. School was in session, and it simply wasn't practical for the kids to miss three weeks of classes, but I still felt pretty guilty for leaving them for weeks on end. Someday, I thought, I'll bring them back here, to this magical place. In the meantime, I took a bit of comfort in getting birthday wishes from them.

33

Rising the next morning, I tried to force down some breakfast on a queasy stomach. My nerves were so raw by now, I was referring to breakfast as "bagels and bile" and "dry heaves and toast." The day started with a long warm-up to Lava, a fourteen-mile flat-water paddle that gave me plenty of time to contemplate what lay ahead.

I tried to conjure up everything that Harlan had been telling me since we first launched, to keep my mind free from clutter and distractions, from doubt and fear, to be at peace with my decisions, and to channel the energy of the river. I tried to remove all the negative thoughts that enveloped my consciousness like silty water invading a clear stream.

About a half mile above Lava Falls, Harlan pointed out Vulcan's Anvil, a fifty-foot plug of basalt, rising straight up out of the middle of the river. "It's the cone of an extinct volcano," he said, "the last remnant of that thousand-foot dam."

One day the river will erode it all and take it downstream, too, I thought.

Harlan told me that the Hualapai and Paiute tribes believed their ancestors met at the top of the anvil to solve disputes. It was a sacred place for them, a center of energy and power.

"In the afternoon light," Rob said, "it looks jet black." I had Rob direct me over to it, and I paddled a symbolic circle around it. As I raised my open palm toward the rock, I could feel its heat, even from a few feet away.

With Lava now booming below us, we pulled over and went ashore to scout, scrambling over the time-hardened lava rocks, river right. Six years of training and 179 miles through the canyon had led me here. In a way I couldn't believe it. The hour had arrived. We stood on an overlook above the rapid, and Harlan took my hand and pointed it across the river to Prospect Canyon, the source of the big boulders that had come down and constricted this section so dramatically. Below us, it sounded catastrophic, like a constant thunderclap, like a place where the earth was angry, roiling and erupting with a million tons of water instead of magma.

"Sounds big," I forced the words out.

"It's definitely big," said Harlan, "but it's just another rapid. Don't go into this any differently than the others, like Upset. Remember what that felt like."

Lonnie was next to me and started talking in an exuberant chatter. "I remember Lava Falls when I had my eyesight, seeing it on *Wide World of Sports*. This raft went in there, hit the Ledge Hole, and flipped. I'll never forget the image of that big ole raft vertical, then upside down, all the rigging tearing out, coolers coming out, people flying out, and that rubber boat doing end-over-end flips."

I tried to picture the Ledge Hole, Lava's most infamous and awe-inspiring feature, a wide rock pour-over producing a wave twelve feet tall and, on the other side, a massive pileup of white water. It was known as the place on the Grand Canyon where you didn't want to be. "The thrill of victory and the agony of defeat," I managed to reply, and then I sank down on a rock.

"When I came through here my last time," Lonnie jumped back in, "I remember standing right here, where we are now, listening to that roar and feeling the vibration through my feet. You feel that? And I'm thinking, Okay, I'm gonna do this. I dropped in, missed the Ledge Hole on the left, got a little squirrelly on the right, flipped and rolled back up, and I'm digging with my paddle like a boll weevil through a tater patch, but I got flipped again, and my spray skirt imploded. I coulda swore it took my legs off. Ripped me right out of my kayak so violently, they told me my boat went flying in the air doing flips, twenty feet in the air. I finally popped up, paddle still in my hands, and one of my guides came and rescued me."

By the time Lonnie had finished recounting his run, I felt dizzy and listless. I thought I was going to puke. I tried to fight the nausea with the proactive breathing exercises Timmy had taught me, but I couldn't seem to breathe it away. I wasn't sure if it was Lonnie's story, the temperature that had topped one hundred degrees, the fourteen-mile paddle that morning, the exhaustion of the last two weeks, or all the pressure and buildup to this moment; maybe it was all of it, but I felt my confidence slipping away and the debris pouring in, constricting the current of my mind, strangling the flow. I could feel the weight of it all, like those obstructions lurking deep below Lava yet profoundly affecting what I would experience on the surface.

Harlan began describing the line, and I needed to maintain my composure. I listened to him as best I could, given the images of tumbling rafts and kayaks spinning through the air. He took my hand again, pointing it along the line. "We're gonna ease in center river right, just to the left of a strong eddy line. There are some really weird, powerful boils coming off the shore. They'll try to surf you to the left. Fight the spin and stay loose and relaxed.

"We'll have the Ledge Hole on our left and some big pour-overs to our right. We'll punch through two pretty sizable surging waves and try to line up for the V-Wave. There are two of them crashing together. The right side's no good. It's a muncher, and behind it is the corner pocket—not a good place to wind up. So we'll charge it angling slightly left to punch through the left side of the V. It's a good hit, so if you get knocked over, you have enough time to roll up before the next features. If you stay upright, then we'll keep angling out into the river, so we avoid my old friend the Cheese Grater Rock. Then we'll straighten out and hit the Big Kahuna waves. There's a series of them, but two big ones. Then you just ride out the tail waves, and we're done."

Through my paddling booties, I could feel the burning lava rock scalding the bottom of my feet. Late afternoon wind whipped up the canyon. My lips were cracked, my throat parched, my tongue chalky.

"Ready to do this, E?" Harlan asked.

"I think so," I replied. I'd never been so terrified in my life.

34

I scrambled down the boulders and climbed into my kayak. Although I'd given up the practice of cranking the ratchets in my cockpit eighteen precise times, I still had a careful pre-paddling ritual that took several minutes and served as meditation. First, I pulled the ropes that tightened my backrest and the bulkhead under my feet. I made sure no folds on my dry top would get hooked over anything that would prevent me from wet exiting if I needed to. I pulled on my neoprene skirt, snapping it over my cockpit from back to front. I slid on my helmet, maneuvered the microphone in front of my lips, and wiggled the earpiece so it was flush against my ear. I buckled the chin strap, making sure there were no twists, wrapped the cord of my comm system around the shoulder strap of my PFD: two loops and tuck the system into the chest pocket. Lastly, I held my paddle out, rolling it in my hands; it was easy to grab it backward, so I carefully felt the paddle blades, noting the feathering and angle. We

turned on the radios. They beeped to indicate they were working. Harlan was fairly clear: "Check, check," I heard. "Small left,
small right, testing, testing."

We pushed into the river. I was floating out, away from anything solid, anything I could hang on to. It was happening. Lava's
terrible bellow grew louder, beginning to cancel all other sound except Harlan's voice. "We're here, right now, in this moment; nothing else matters. Be clear and calm and concise."

But unlike Upset Rapid where my actions had felt crisp and
fluid, and my surroundings had slowed, now it was my body moving slowly with the canyon racing by. My movements felt labored,
my muscles stiff and tense. I felt the power of the current beneath
my hull as it hurled me toward Lava's tongue. I wanted to put on
the brakes and pull over, to rethink what I was doing, but there
was no time.

"We're about a hundred yards above now," Harlan said. "Small
left. Hold that line." I tried to execute his command, but my re-
sponse time felt seconds behind, and my paddle strokes felt mushy,
like I was disconnected from the water. "Small left again. Hold that
line. Right there. Nice calm strokes; good thoughtful strokes. Hold
that line."

I silently repeated our familiar mantra: "Relax. Breathe. Be at
peace with the river."

His voice became louder, more urgent. "Approaching those
boils . . . fight the spin, fight the spin." I was struck simultaneously
from the right-side boils and the surging main left channel, but as
I dug in with my paddle blade, fighting those invisible hands
grabbing my bow, I reverted to a bad habit I thought I'd broken
two years ago. I felt my upper body lean the wrong way, and I was

instantly upside down, with no idea which direction my boat was pointing.

My mind swirled like the current above and below me, like a blind man's version of a fun house, bombarded by mirrors, no sense of space or direction. I'd accepted the fact that I'd probably flip somewhere in Lava, but I would never have imagined being upside down heading into it. How could this even be happening?

It would have been comical if it weren't so insanely scary. I managed to get my paddle to the surface, snap my hips, and roll back up to the growl of the river. I heard Harlan yelling "Hard left!" then instantly "Hard right!" and I tried to respond, but my reactions and movements were imprecise. My speed increased as I jostled and pitched over the entry waves and plunged down a slope into what had to be the V-Wave, then felt a collision like hitting a solid wall. My boat was thrown up and backward as I flipped again. My kayak spun above me as I managed to roll up once more, now hyperventilating.

Harlan's words came fast and loud now: "Left! You're good! You're good!" But I wasn't good. I could feel the current tugging me backward toward a deafening roar, like giant breakers pounding a beach. I was pointing backward going into the Kahuna waves. "Hard right!" Harlan yelled. "Charge! Charge!" But I couldn't get around in time.

An enormous wave broke over me from behind, hitting me in the back of the helmet, knocking my body forward, and yanking my kayak down and under. My arms felt paralyzed as I was buried in an avalanche of water. Then I was over again, tumbling and gyroscoping under all that weight, the opposing currents violently grabbing at my paddle blades, trying to rip it from my hands. Somehow I rolled up in the midst of the storm, but there was no direction from Harlan. Then another wave hammered me from my left, and I fought to brace. I took a gasp of half air and foam as I went under again.

The howling roar became an underwater gurgle of exploding bubbles. Waves pounded my boat from above, bashing me down harder as each of my roll attempts got weaker. At last I was out of air, and I desperately reached for my grab loop and yanked, popping my spray skirt and launching myself out of my boat.

I clawed for the surface, for air, inhaling water as more waves slammed down and spun and shook me. My head finally popped above the surface, and I gasped for breath. I could hear voices again—Rob's? Timmy's?—but not Harlan's as I felt a boat next to me and held on to it, trying to catch hold of something; it tipped a little, like the beginning of an Eskimo roll. I realized then I was feeling a smooth hull, the bottom of a boat. It was Harlan. He'd flipped, too! I let go, and Timmy was beside me, hauling me toward an eddy.

Then I could hear Harlan again, his voice breathless and quavering, explaining that a big wave had snapped his carbon fiber paddle in half, the severed, jagged edge spearing him in the face. That's why he'd flipped. But I was hardly listening as Timmy deposited me on shore and I pulled myself up onto the slippery rocks at the river's edge, thankful to be out of that terrifying maelstrom.

I could hear my team's voices and their boats clacking into one another as they hovered in the eddy. Rob said, "You're done, buddy. No more big rapids."

With shaking hands, I took off my helmet. Water and silt streamed down my face as I tried to process what had just happened.

"No worries, Erik," Harlan said. "You remember that old kayaking adage, right? We're all just between swims."

As I sat there, I tried to keep my face from reacting, trying to hide the shock and devastation. Lonnie ran Lava clean, flipping just once. The team whooped and hooted for his success, especially since he'd swum last year. I cheered for him, too, but not with as much enthusiasm as I should have. I felt bitter, like I'd let my team and myself down. It felt as if I had dishonored the journey I was on.

35

We pulled off and camped at Tequila Beach just a half mile below, beside the rapid called Son of Lava. The boys tried to cheer me up, and Harlan said, "Look at it this way. Right now, you are as far from Lava Falls as you could possibly be. You are through it. Lava is behind you."

He was right in a way. Swimming through one rapid didn't make the entire trip a failure. In the overall scheme of things, it didn't really matter that I swam. I was through it. I was safe. I was alive. Part of me was glad it was over.

It was a bitter relief. Now I could get on with it, move downriver, and never have to think about it again, but if that was the case, why did I feel a plaguing regret and a vague sense of possibilities unfulfilled? How were you supposed to know when to let go and when to hang on? When to let the river take you downstream toward something new and when to double back? I turned in early that night, exhausted, defeated, and confused.

Son of Lava rumbled outside my tent door. I listened carefully
for a long time to its ebb and flow as waves built and curled and
crashed down again; currents swirled, clashed, and mingled, and
the water relentlessly churned and pounded over rocks. Everything, I thought, had a subtext, a language hidden beneath. I tried
to understand what the river was saying, but was I wise enough to
decipher it?

I had believed, perhaps naively, that if you committed to something, if you trained hard enough, if you believed strongly enough,
the barriers would open up before you like floodgates and you'd
be treated to a glorious and well-earned storybook ending. Even
through all the struggle and anxiety, the bleeding and shortfalls,
I had secretly and stubbornly clung to this premise. Yet it hadn't
ended that way, far from it. I had dreamed I would emerge changed
in some way, strengthened by the journey. I'd wanted to flourish
in the river, like Harlan; it had become a part of his mind and soul.
Yet I still felt separated, like I was navigating in an alien landscape.

I had swum through Lava, blind, frantic, bathed in fear, and
emerged on the other end like a drowned rat. What did you learn
from that, except that life was to be endured, to be survived?

"Don't let that be the culmination!" I spoke aloud to my empty
tent.

As I continued to toss and turn, the river seemed so loud, I
could barely hear the group still reveling outside. Their voices were
muted, droning into the night. The river, I thought, represented
those massive forces bigger than me, bigger than all of us: that
crushing diagnosis that radically altered the course of your life, the
catastrophic event that changed the course of history, the adversity that knocked you down and defied you to get up again. Blind-

ness was one of them. There was absolutely nothing I could have done in the face of it. Death was another. But misery, depression, disillusionment, alienation, fear: They were all second cousins. They rushed forward, splintering, pulverizing, disintegrating everything in their path, and we pretended we could somehow affect that unyielding trajectory.

Even Harlan, who had achieved a level of mastery I still had trouble imagining, had been spit out the bottom of Lava, upside down, his paddle snapped in half and his nose almost broken. No. Humans were not the driving force, I thought. We were more like rocks in the river or the canyon walls, being scoured and eroded by circumstances and time. And I was powerless in the face of that energy.

But as those ideas and doubts flooded through my brain, there were persistent examples, a number of outliers, people who seemed to run counter to the theory. Rob was one of them. I remembered him on the Usumacinta, beaten down by the effects of cancer, his spine fractured, yet paddling furiously toward a drowning teammate and saving his life. His cancer had been a kind of challenge he'd never confronted before, yet, despite that, he bravely went forward to live fully and confront the uncertainty that lay ahead.

There were many other examples, too. To name just a few, there was my old friend Mark Wellman, who had broken his back yet had climbed El Capitan. He'd performed a kind of alchemy, turning lead into gold. Kyle Maynard had pioneered what seemed impossible and, with a great team around him, crabbed his way to the top of Kilimanjaro. Mandy Harvey had done something preposterous by learning to let go and write and sing music she would never hear.

It occurred to me that all these friends had something in common: Their actions were counterintuitive, defying the reality of what they saw and felt. They grew rather than diminished. They went in unlikely directions, instead of accepting safety and stagnation.

And Terry Fox was always at the top of my list. Despite all the evidence pointing toward futility, he had chosen to run thousands of miles across a continent. He would never live to witness the results of his heroic act, yet he had done it anyway, and that choice had made all the difference.

If my life had anything in common with a rapid, it made sense that there was a map, one that was even harder to read than the one on a river. These people had illuminated parts of that map, had lit up the path like contrails in the sky, like bioluminescence in dark water. It was a map I desperately yearned to build and follow. And the choices I made would either paralyze me, send me spiraling into a whirlpool, or propel me forward, admittedly in crazy and unexpected ways.

It was staggeringly difficult, however, not to see the overpowering evidence of the world, and use it as validation to protect yourself, and to shut down. It took such relentless trust in your team, in what lay ahead, to stay open to the possibilities that existed like a blank canvas, or like the infinite sky that gave promise to those features that could be touched, heard, and seen.

I could still hear Harlan in my ear, reminding me to have faith that the journey down the river was a good one.

36

Without much sleep, the next day, I crawled out of my tent. I heard soft voices and found Harlan and Rob already awake. They were next to the kayaks, talking quietly. I approached, swinging my trekking pole in front of me, and realized Timmy, Skyler, and Steven were there, too. I pulled Harlan aside and said, "What do you say we . . . maybe . . . try it again."

"You know," he replied, "I've been thinking the same thing. In fact, I was hoping you'd say that." It was unanimous. Everyone agreed and began quietly suiting up. Lava Falls was one of the few major rapids on the Grand Canyon that you could actually portage around upstream and run again. So even though it felt backward, Harlan, Rob, Timmy, Steven, Skyler, and I began carrying our boats toward the top of Lava, wordlessly bushwhacking through the thick tamarisk scrub. This time, although the rapid was just as loud as it had been the day before, it sounded less menacing, and I felt calm.

Just below Lava, the navigable terrain ended, and we had to cross the river to reach the top of the rapid. As I paddled across the squirrelly water below the tail waves, I flipped over in the clash of the eddy line and struggled to roll up again. I got up on my second try, and as soon as my head rose above water, I could hear the crash of Lava above. Again, I felt that panic shoot through my body like lightning.

"I'm having second thoughts," I said. "Maybe I should rethink this." But the team ignored me and kept paddling. I knew that was their way of spurring me on. Soon we were across to the other side. Everyone grabbed their boats and kept trudging along the shoreline upstream. I followed. We finally dropped the boats at the put-in, and Timmy lightened the mood by enthusiastically proclaiming, "It's time to get a little bit of Lava 2.0!"

Then everyone was quiet again. I climbed into my boat and sat for a couple of minutes, listening to Lava below me. It was still cranking. Maybe it was impossible to fight those forces, I thought, to go toe to toe with them. They were just too big and powerful. There were moments to paddle against the flow, to reposition, but as Harlan had been repeating, there were also moments to ride the current, to harness the energy of the river and move with it. On Upset, I'd felt that synchronicity, and I'd assumed that once you experienced it, you would carry it permanently. Yet it dawned on me that such connection wasn't acquired once and then owned forever. That flow, that fusion of water and landscape and light—it was something that you had to constantly strive for. It was about struggling and flailing to find it once, and then again and again and again. And it would always be waiting.

I slid off the rocks, my boat slapping the water, and I was racing again toward the throat of Lava. Harlan's voice was just as it had been at Upset Rapid—a kind of melding with my thoughts. I committed to feeling and reacting instead of thinking, letting my body move with the current. As I headed down the tongue, beneath the butterflies, beneath the anticipation, I felt gratitude for whatever the river would take from me, or whatever it would give.

My second run wasn't dramatically different from my first. I paddled just beside the right eddy line and hit the same boils, braced as I'd done before. I felt myself going over. This time, though, I consciously willed myself to lean and lift the edge of my kayak. I bobbled for a precarious second and then shot by into the entry waves. Again, the V-Wave knocked me backward. I flipped but stuck my roll, angling farther out into the river to line up against the next test.

My entry into the Big Kahuna waves was far from ideal. I didn't quite get around and got slammed sideways. I rolled up, enveloped by collapsing water and foam, and was knocked over again. But this time I stayed calm, closed my eyes, and surrendered to the chaos as the roiling forces flipped and spun me around.

Then the water stilled around me. My roll came easily, and I felt myself bobbing down the bottom of the Big Kahunas with Harlan's jubilant voice yelling, "You're through! You're through! You did it!"

That night, Seth, one of Lonnie's guides, presented me with a drawing he'd been working on at various camps. He described it to me as a dark river cutting through a deep canyon. "The boils," he said, "often the worst when least expected, represent

the unpredictability and hardship of the expedition. The imposing walls, massive and confining, forced us to confront our
greatest challenges and our greatest discoveries."

Penned across one of Seth's canyon walls was a poem, written
by Katie Proctor, one of our AzRA guides. She read it aloud:

Some say seeing is believing.
> But I've been a witness.
> To truth being felt.
> The unseen is understood when experienced.
> The open-heart policy.
> Paddle in hand.
> Each stroke leaving a wake of inspiration behind like currents
>   expanding out to distant shores.
> You will never know the magnitude of their impression.
> The momentum of possibility.
> You will not be eddied out in your quest for experiencing the
>   fullness of current.
> Strange how having the courage to live from a place of nonsense
>   can lead to the living of your wildest dreams.
> Through the journey, children will ask you about faith.
> Just trust and ah . . . give it a whirl.

On September 27, 277 miles after putting in at Lees Ferry, our team
rounded the final river bend, and I could hear the canyon walls
shrinking and widening as the Grand Wash Cliffs gave way to the
Nevada desert above Lake Mead. My mind swirled with conflict-
ing emotions and memories from the river as our paddle strokes
cleaved the smooth water. Harlan called out his final commands

to me—"Small right. Hold that line"—and I heard his voice crack a little. I thought he might be crying. Then my boat touched the shore, and, as I climbed out onto the sandy beach, I heard soft, smiling voices.

"Hi, Dad."

"Arjun? Emma?" I now fully understood the source or Harlan's tears. I began crying, too, as I reached out and swept them up in my arms. Ellie then stepped forward and joined the embrace, her warm voice whispering congratulations in my ear.

Then we were all hugging and swaying together. That's when I understood the source of Harlan's tears. He'd been bearing a lot during that last stretch as he saw my family waiting silently and expectantly on the beach. He'd also been carrying a burden throughout the entire project. He'd taken on the daunting responsibility of guiding me down a river that had once nearly taken his life, and he'd delivered me safely into the arms of my family, from his home, and now back to mine.

EPILOGUE

Since the completion of the Grand Canyon expedition, the team has been charging forward in characteristic style. Lonnie "the LonDart" Bedwell outdid his accomplishment on the Grand Canyon by heading to Zambia with Timmy O'Neill and famous kayaker Eric Jackson. Together they paddled a twenty-five-mile section of the Zambezi River with rapids even bigger and fiercer than those of the Grand Canyon. When I asked him if he was scared of the crocs, he answered, "I wasn't too worried. If one came at me, I was told to paddle straight at it, and they usually duck. Then, of course, you turn around and paddle like hell!"

Lonnie still hunts with the man who accidentally shot him, and he recently organized a turkey hunt in Indiana for blind and visually impaired veterans. "Hunting blind," he says. "Why not?"

But topping all of his accomplishments, he finally took a leap and bought a cell phone. Although last time I called him, I got this voice message: "Hey, you've reached Lonnie. Thanks for calling. I'll call you back as soon as I can see to find the phone."

For Steven Mace, our expedition became a launching point. He distinguished himself as such a valuable hard worker, he was subsequently hired as a guide for Arizona Raft Adventures and now works in the Big Ditch.

When I asked Timmy O'Neill what he was going to do after the Grand Canyon, he said, "Continue to live a life of chaos, rebellion, mystery, and love." For his fortieth birthday, he BASE jumped off El Capitan and Half Dome in one day, and he continues to push the boundaries of climbing and slacklining. In honor of his brother Sean, who was paralyzed, he helped found Paradox Sports, with a mission of promoting adaptive mountain sports. Most recently he's been volunteering with the Himalayan Cataract Project in developing countries like Ethiopia, assisting in eye surgeries to cure preventable blindness.

While poring over river maps of Peru, Rocky Contos made a remarkable discovery. The Apurímac in Peru had been established as the most distant source of the Amazon, but after careful examination, he determined that the nearby Río Mantaro was actually eighty kilometers longer. Not wanting to miss out, Rocky scrambled to put together a plan and headed for South America. After hiking for two days to the headwaters of the Río Mantaro, Rocky spent the next two months kayaking and traveling by boat, becoming the first person ever to complete the entire descent of the Amazon from its most distant source to the sea.

Rob Raker was diagnosed with Stage IV prostate cancer in 2010, but he has outlived the initial prognosis and is still going strong. In February 2016, Rob was accepted into a clinical trial at the

National Institutes of Health, a treatment involving a genetically tailored vaccine that could help his immune system fight the cancer. Since February 2016, his PSA has stopped increasing.

Just before Rob's sixty-first birthday, his dear friend Steve Edwards died of cancer. Steve was a fitness legend who helped develop P90X and was known for creating grueling birthday challenges. To honor Steve's life, Rob devised one of his own:

In 61 hours over the next 6.1 days I will attempt to:

—Photograph 61 different species of birds
—Ski downhill 61,000 vertical feet
—Bike and hike 61 miles
—Run 6.1 miles
—Do 61 push-ups each of the six days
—Do 61 sit-ups each of the six days
—Rock climb 610 vertical feet at 5.10 or higher difficulty . . .

And try to have fun doing it all.

Harlan Taney spends as much time as possible in the Grand Canyon. Based out of Flagstaff, Arizona, his company, 4 Corner Film Logistics, has worked with the BBC on a reenactment of the Powell Expedition, a production on the condors of the Vermilion Cliffs, and projects to save the Grand Canyon from proposed megadevelopment. "It's a wild and sacred place," said Harlan, "one of the Natural Wonders of the World, and I intend to keep it that way." Recently, while working on a conservation film in the canyon, Harlan had a revelation. "The Grand Canyon," he said, "is only one of countless threatened environments around the world, and media content could be a powerful tool to preserve them all." As a result, he recently founded an organization to capture video footage of natural habitats that are endangered worldwide and archive them in an open-source database—all to create awareness for their protection. As Harlan excitedly told me the news, I remembered the story of his first trip down the Grand Canyon as a little boy, and I pictured other children tossing sticks into other sacred and wild rivers, watching them drift away, and having the chance to dream about where they go.

Besides my kayaking team, there were so many others whose lives had intersected with mine over the last fifteen years. It was quite a list.

For Kyle Maynard, making history on Kilimanjaro wasn't quite enough. On February 21, 2016, Kyle crawled to the summit of Aconcagua, at 22,841 feet the highest point in South America.

Emma continues to volunteer at a rescue organization for stray dogs and cats. She's now fostered and found homes for seventy dogs. Notably, one, whom she named Duncan, was cracked in the head with a mallet soon after birth by his owner and thrown in a trash can. Somehow he lived. When Emma received the dog, he had a dent in his skull and stared straight ahead. Duncan had to be guided to his food and water dish. Yet with love and care, one week later, his tail was wagging, and he was running and barking in the backyard. Emma said, "Hey, Dad, Duncan is a No Barriers dog."

Ellie continues to be my greatest ally. Not only has she tolerated me over the years as I've delivered flowers with the petals all disintegrated after an unexpected downpour, washed dishes with syrup instead of dish soap (the bottles feel remarkably similar), or gone to dinner with one black shoe and one brown, she also pilots our tandem bike, and guides me on skis. Through our family's Reach Foundation, Ellie administers several scholarships for children throughout Nepal.

After playing in a recreational soccer league for a season, Arjun made a bold decision to pursue a spot on the A team again. At the tryouts he made several textbook crosses that resulted in goals. Ellie said the three coaches were observing and scribbling notes in their booklets. A few days later, Arjun was invited onto the A team, where he excels.

We managed to find Arjun's birth mom, Kanchi, in Nepal, and have maintained contact with her ever since. We set her up with fuel, wax, and wicks to start her own candle business. Because of Kathmandu's frequent power outages, candles are in high demand. She makes about fifty pounds of candles a day, and when she sells them all, she makes much more than she did working construction. When Arjun turned sixteen, we returned to Nepal to visit her.

We held our eighth No Barriers Summit at Copper Mountain, Colorado. As I stood on the stage about to speak at the closing ceremony, I could hear the murmur of the audience in front of me, a thousand people of diverse backgrounds and circumstances: people with physical disabilities, as well as those who struggled with obesity, brain injuries, and PTSD. There were those who'd survived cancer, strokes, addiction, and physical and emotional trauma. Surprisingly, lots of ordinary families had also joined our community, as well as CEOs and corporate leaders, who had taken the No Barriers principles and were applying them to their teams and organizations. Lastly, there were everyday people who just felt lost, or suffered from fear, anxiety, and self-doubt.

I could feel the energy under the Colorado sky as I began to speak: "It was while climbing a desert tower years ago with Mark Wellman and Hugh Herr," I started, "that I first asked myself, is there something that unites our experience? Whether you're blind, missing legs, or unable to walk—like the three of us—or whether you're a veteran who comes home feeling alienated and depressed, or a parent struggling to lead her family, or a kid whose barrier is that he's never been more than a mile from his house, or a teen in the suburbs who has no idea how to impact her world, or someone trying to grow a new idea into something magnificent. What is the glue that binds all of us together, every human who lives and breathes? Are there tools, ideas . . . is there a mind-set, a light inside that we can all access—to equip us for that journey?

"The answer has led us all here, to this movement that we are building. And what is the fundamental message of this movement? I wish it were as simple as a motivational slogan like, 'If you believe it, you can achieve it,' but life is not a storybook, and its lessons can seem shifting and contradictory. Our paths can lead us toward suffering, yet sometimes, toward the beginnings of change."

The wind picked up and blew down from the mountain slopes and through the village. I could hear the No Barriers flags, hung from the stage, fluttering in the breeze.

"When I first started paddling into whitewater rapids, they appeared to me as utter chaos, but I found that if you pay close attention, and listen very carefully, you can discover a hidden map. Kayakers call this the line. It's hard to read and decipher. It's even harder to navigate. But if you manage to follow it, or even to get close, you can find a way through. That map, that line, that discovery, is what we call 'No Barriers.'"

For more information, go to www.erikweihenmayer.com.

GLOSSARY

anaerobic when the body doesn't have enough oxygen

basalt dense metamorphic rock dark gray to black in color

bioluminescence the light made by some deep-sea creatures

bow the forward part of a boat

bulkhead a wall that creates a storage area in a kayak

canyon a deep and narrow valley with steep sides and often with a body of water running through it

cascade falling, rushing water

cfs cubic feet per second, a unit used to measure the flow of water

chasm a deep opening in the surface of the earth

cleft an opening

cockpit the part of a kayak where someone sits

conquistadors Spanish soldiers out to conquer lands and people

contrail streaks created in the sky by airplanes or rockets

deforestation the process of forests being cut down

ducky an inflatable kayak

eddy   a current of water running differently—often circular—from the main current of water

erode   to wear away by water

flotilla   a line of boats

glacier   a large body of ice on land

gorge   a narrow passage through land, such as a part of a canyon

gyroscoping   spinning rapidly

hole   a feature created by water flowing over an obstacle on or near the river surface

hydraulic   of or related to water

lateral   of or related to the side

maelstrom   a powerful, often violent commotion

mesa   a flat-topped natural elevation

neoprene skirt   waterproof material that fits over the cockpit of a kayak

paraplegic   someone who is paralyzed below the waist

petroglyph   a carving on a rock

pictograph   an ancient drawing on a rock wall

portage   to carry a boat and other goods from one part of a body of water to another

prosthetics   artificial body parts

quadriplegic   someone who is either completely or partially paralyzed in both the arms and legs

raft   a flat structure used for transportation on the water

riffle   rough water

schist   parallel layers of flaky rock

scree   loose stones and rocks on or at the base of a hill

sediment   matter that settles to the bottom of a liquid

silt   grainy material deposits in a river

strainer an obstacle in a river that only limited amounts of water can pass through

switchback a zigzag road or trail

tempest a violent storm

terrain a piece of land

tributary a stream feeding a larger body of water

trough low part of a wave

turbulence agitation

velocity speed

wave train a series of waves

whirlpool water moving in a circle and drawing in floating objects

ACKNOWLEDGMENTS

Erik: I just returned from a climb of Crestone Needle, an eighteen-hour summit day with a treacherous descent. For hours upon hours, I faced the rock, down-climbing with vast space behind me. My friends took turns, just below me, spotting me and giving me constant directions, saying where to grab and where to place my feet. When I reflect on their patience and dedication, it gives me chills to realize how fortunate I am to have such extraordinary teams in my life. Without these people, the course of my life would have been dramatically different. So I'd like to honor my great teams over the years, those allies who have rallied around the dreams of a blind man.

First, thanks to my Mount Everest team who defied the naysayers to help me make history in 2001, and especially our team leader, Pasquale. You challenged me not to make Everest the "greatest thing I ever do."

To Uncle Rob, aka "Papa Duck," I'm deeply grateful. You started me on my Grand Canyon journey and taught me so much about kayaking and friendship. Rob was also instrumental during the entire writing process. His archived photography, excellent memory, and acute attention to detail were indispensable throughout.

Harlan, thanks for keeping your eyes on me and helping me to navigate through the storm. You opened your heart, home, and family to us and brought such depth and passion to the project—it's been inspiring to get to know you.

Many thanks to my entire No Barriers Grand Canyon team for helping me to prepare and build the confidence to take on the challenge.

Skyler and my Touch the Top team, you make things happen behind the scenes and never get enough credit. I want you to know you rock.

To Dave and the staff at No Barriers, you bring our movement to life and are the alchemy behind the mission.

Thanks to Gail for championing this project, and to Laurie for believing in me twice now.

Love and appreciation to my dad, Ed, for recounting some wonderful family stories. I can still remember the roar of your A-4 Skyhawk swooping over our house in Hightstown and rattling the windows. Semper Fi.

A big bear hug to my bro, Eddi, for reminding us about his insane four-wheeling adventures with our brother Mark, the hot peppers, and "Down in Orlando . . . !" We love you, Mark.

My deepest gratitude goes to my wife, Ellie, who read every page of the manuscript with care, diligence, and love. You sat awake many nights giving critical feedback that guided the book and its themes. You're the real writer of the family, and I couldn't have done this without you.

Thank you to Buddy Levy, my coauthor. We met in 2003 at an adventure race in Greenland when he was covering the event as a journalist. For several days, Buddy was embedded with my team, and he made the grueling miles go a little faster with his thought-provoking questions and sense of humor that lifted our exhaustion and made us belly-laugh along the trail.

Buddy: I watched in amazement as Erik paddled through iceberg-filled fjords, bushwhacked over boulder-strewn terrain, rode a tandem mountain bike at frightening speeds, and summited numerous peaks. I already knew that he'd summited Mount Everest and was impressed by his mountaineering résumé, but tromping through Greenland with him, I came to know his humor, his determination, and his vision for obliterating barriers. I stayed in contact with Erik over the next decade, writing a number of magazine articles about him, going skiing with him, and getting to know his family. In 2013, I went to my first No Barriers Summit, and there experienced firsthand the unique assemblage of people connected by a shared philosophy, which is the No Barrier's motto: "What's Within You Is Stronger Than What's in Your Way."

I was fortunate to be invited on Erik's historic "kayaking blind" journey down the Grand Canyon in September 2014. At camp one late afternoon, we began discussing the idea of coauthoring a book about his life since descending from the summit of Mount Everest. Without really knowing exactly how we'd pull it off, we embarked on a very ambitious project together. There were moments near our final deadline when it felt like I'd been in a tiny tent on a mountainside with Erik for an entire year. It was a slog, and we worked long, hard, sometimes hair-pulling hours together. In the end, I have become as impressed by Erik's intellectual capacities, his vision and his philosophies about life, as I have been by his athletic accomplishments. He is a transformative person, and it's been an honor to be involved at such an intimate level with his story, his family, and his team. So thanks to Erik for entrusting me to help tell this remarkable story and for taking me along on this incredible journey.

Thanks especially to the Weihenmayer family for always making me feel at home on my visits, and making me feel like a part of the family.

My dear friend John Larkin has been a first reader on all of my books and he gave his honest, attentive, and sage wisdom on every page of the *No Barriers* book. *Muchas gracias*, Juan!

Also, cheers to my dear Free Range Writers, who are always with me.

Finally, to my wife, Camie, and my children, Logan and Hunter—your ceaseless support buoys me when I'm flailing in rough waters. You allow me to do what I most love: write stories.

ABOUT THE AUTHORS

Skyler Williams

ERIK WEIHENMAYER is an athlete, adventurer, motivational speaker, and the bestselling author of *Touch the Top of the World* and *The Adversity Advantage*. He cofounded No Barriers USA, which empowers people to break through barriers, find their inner purpose, and contribute their very best to the world. Erik lives in Colorado.

BUDDY LEVY is an author, educator, journalist, and speaker. His books include *Labyrinth of Ice, Conquistador, River of Darkness, Geronimo,* and *American Legend.* He is a clinical professor of English at Washington State University. He lives in Idaho.